By SARIA BRYANT

ELEMENTAL THRONES
Shadow's Wound
Wild's Scar

UNDERWORLD MAGES
Mage's Marines
Mage's Fugitive

TOUCH OF LEATHER
If You Let Me

Published by DREAMSPINNER PRESS
www.dreamspinnerpress.com

SARIA BRYANT

MAGE'S FUGITIVE

REAMSPINNER
PRESS

Published by

DREAMSPINNER PRESS

8219 Woodville Hwy #1245
Woodville, FL 32362 USA
www.dreamspinnerpress.com

Mage's Fugitive
© 2025 Saria Bryant

Cover Art
© 2025 Andrei Bat
https://99designs.com/profiles/bandrei
Cover content is for illustrative purposes only and any person depicted on the cover is a model.

Trade Paperback ISBN: 9781641088589
Digital ISBN: 9781641088572
Trade Paperback published December 2025
v. 1.0

Dedication: To the aces.

Acknowledgements

Special thanks to Deianira for her patience in letting me pick her brain on Hmong culture and shamanism. Any mistakes in representation are my own, and some liberties were taken with the magical elements in order to fit the world. I hope you enjoy reading as much as I enjoyed writing this one.

CHAPTER 1

IN LESS than twelve hours, Rían would finally be free of the Order.

One last mission. One final, questionably legal task for the people who had legally abducted him when he was ten. He counted himself lucky his magic hadn't Sparked until after the laws were updated to prevent the Order from taking kids even younger than that. The fact they'd been able to secure their position as the sole authority for training and governing mages, outside of Japan and a few smaller countries, was the result of centuries of manipulation and countless billions of various currencies into corrupt channels.

He'd daydreamed hundreds of ways to make the Order's empire crumble, but he wasn't stupid enough to give voice to any of those plans, much less try to enact them alone.

He squinted at his laptop screen as he looked through apartments. After tonight, he'd officially be homeless. If he survived. Not that he was too worried about it; he did have a place he could use in the meantime.

No, he was more annoyed at the fact that all of his careful planning over the last year was now moot, courtesy of a certain shifter pack and their new mage.

Denver had been a magical dead zone for the last few decades, ever since the shifter massacre there fifty years ago. It didn't seem to be common knowledge even among other mages, but there was a definite link between shifters inhabiting an area and the number of mages who Sparked there. No shifters meant no mages, but the moment Caius and his pack declared their intentions to claim territory there, boom. Magic.

Rían had been hoping to live there for years without needing to worry about the Order swooping in to kidnap young mages, as they were wont to do. Now he had to choose between dealing with the Order for the rest of his life and setting up shop in a major city with more mages for competition instead, or looking for another dead zone. The fact he'd already signed a lease for a building and hired a crew to put his tattoo shop together meant he'd lose a decent chunk of money if he went somewhere else, but the loss could be worth it.

Niamh, his sugar glider familiar, barked from her perch on the bed, letting him know it was time to go.

"Yeah, yeah," he muttered as he shut his laptop and shoved it into its bag. Even after fourteen years stuck here, most of his everyday possessions fit into a few bags. His magical tools and supplies in one, his laptop in another, and a few changes of clothes and some knickknacks in another. The first was by far the largest.

He glanced around the small room, barely large enough for a bed and a desk, that he'd lived in for most of his life and resisted the urge to set it on fire. He wouldn't be looking back, that was for certain, though he expected the Order to have some underhanded ploy ready when he finished this last mission. They weren't ones for letting their mages go so easily, even after they'd served their time.

Apparently he was needed in a village in Brazil, where the last several months of unrest were threatening to turn into something bigger. The greed of the local village head, Manuel, was threatening to interrupt the Order's supply of biolume shrooms, a fungus more commonly known as Satan's jellyfish due to its volatile qualities that only grew within a small section of the rainforest. Ironic that the Order had put the man in place to begin with years ago to facilitate their access to the jellyfish.

Now Rían was being sent to clean up the mess, and he was allowed to solve the situation with extreme prejudice. Usually that would mean he was ordered to quell the locals, not that orders meant much when he couldn't be forced, but as the villagers were the only ones with the knowledge and skills to quickly and efficiently harvest the Order's precious fungus, Rían was able to finish his last mission on a high note.

He moved to the door of his closet and pressed his hand against it to call his "safe house." Truthfully, it wasn't exactly a house at all, but his Sidhe, one of the few fairy mounds left in existence. His grandmother had access to one that had served their family for generations, but this one had come to him in his first days after the Order abducted him. When he'd been angry and lost and wanting his mother. He'd run through the halls looking for an exit, only to step through a door and onto the rolling green hills of home.

He still remembered the cloying scent of sweet grasses and flowers and the warmth of his mother's cooking. The relief hadn't lasted long, before his family scolded him for running from the Order.

He hadn't been home since, but occasionally he'd find spell components or a new grimoire in his Sidhe, and he knew they'd come from his grandmother.

With a quick glance inside to ensure nothing was out of place, he tossed all but his bag of casting supplies through and closed the door. Then, since he had no intention of stepping into this room ever again, he broke the decade-old link on the door that allowed him to call his Sidhe with a simple touch of his hand.

That done, he opened a portal to the location he'd been given, the outline of a door shimmering a translucent blue in the air. Then, for the first time since his first few solo missions, he hesitated. He wasn't naive enough to think that the mages who disappeared after their last mission were living happily ever after. Far too many died tragically on what was to be their last mission for him to believe this wasn't a trap, but he'd researched all the information as thoroughly as he could. He'd even hidden a few scrying mirrors in the forest around the village the moment he received what was supposed to be his final mission, but there'd been no suspicious movements. No traces of magic aside from what was there naturally.

Nothing was out of the ordinary, but then the final missions of others hadn't been either.

He could only hope all his training paid off and he could handle whatever was waiting for him.

With a deep breath he stepped through into a hot, humid evening in the heart of the rainforest.

He was sweating within moments.

Niamh barked quietly as she landed on his shoulder, and he reflexively checked the pouch around his neck to ensure his other sugar glider had made it with him. The only male in the litter he'd rescued had a penchant for disappearing and making Rían's life difficult. When he spotted the white fur of the albino inside, he breathed a soft sigh of relief and let the doorway vanish.

He turned around to get his bearings, but there was nothing but trees, trees, and more trees. With the time difference between Brazil and Austria, he stepped back in time from early morning to dead of night, and the only light came from the stars and full moon. As his lungs adjusted to the thick, heavy air of his new environment, he welcomed the respite that came with the void of nature. No electricity buzzing beneath his hearing. No press of other bodies nearby. Best of all, no living auras filling his vision. Only the quiet drone of night insects and the green-tinged darkness swallowing him.

Niamh chirped, and Rían turned again, catching the flicker of human auras in the distance.

"Right," he muttered and headed towards the village. He didn't have a plan—he rarely had time to put one together—but he'd figure it out when he got a better look at what he was dealing with. As he drew closer, he saw it was a small village, barely large enough for fifty people to live there, all residing in thatched houses raised off the ground.

Farther back was a small modern villa, and he could see why the villagers here were ready to riot. The audacity of the building itself, with its stone flooring, glass walls, and soft orange lights, was a stark and blatant middle finger to the other villagers living nearby.

He stepped into the village, meeting the startled gazes of the few villagers who saw him. All their auras were faded, with pale lines of stress and anger, most with signs of poor health. Overworked and underfed. He hated how often he saw those markers on his missions.

He motioned to the opulent house in the distance and asked in Portuguese, "Where is the one you want dead?"

A young woman made a startled noise and stepped closer, fear sparking in her aura as she raised a small hatchet covered with the blue bioluminescent glow of the fungus they harvested.

Rían lifted his palm before she could strike. "I'm here to take care of him for you."

She stopped with a wary look, but she lowered her weapon. "He's inside," she said slowly with a jerk of her chin to the villa. "Most likely eating. Again."

He shook his head and headed for the cleared path leading from the village, though he stopped when he passed a large crate full of

Satan's jellyfish. A single one was worth several thousand dollars, but he didn't need the money. They were far more useful to him as ingredients. He'd stocked up on the rarer components as best he could over the past few months, knowing he'd lose the Order's unlimited access to anything he could ever possibly need, but the jellyfish had such a small harvest area that the Order tended to monitor their supply more closely than others. He pulled out a pair of tongs and a large jar from his bag and stuffed seven mushrooms into it. That should last him months if not a year.

Then he continued on, picking his way along the footpath. He was nearing the villa's door and in need of a plan when he felt a ripple of seeking magic. A familiar enough sensation, since the Order liked to keep an eye on all their mages, but this one gave him pause. Rarely did someone seek him out until a day or two after he started a mission.

The silver spiral amulet on his wrist flared, intercepting the spell and redirecting it to the small crystal left under the bed in his room. The crystal acted as a decoy, and whoever cast the seeking spell would be informed Rían was in the room and not the middle of the rainforest.

The basic wards on the home flared bright against his eyes as he approached, and he squinted as he studied them. When he didn't see any hidden traps, he reached into his bag and pulled out his jar of twisted clover. He pinched his nose against the pungent odor and quickly whispered the words to coax the magic of the clover to pierce the ward.

Brown smoke oozed across the bright glow, eating through the protections like acid. When the hole was big enough for him to pass through, he hurried inside, sealed the jar, and shoved it back in his bag. The solid wood door was locked, but a simple spell removed the door entirely and dropped it several feet away.

Niamh leapt off his shoulder and glided across the room. When she reached the end to turn the corner, she chirped in surprise and rebounded off the wall before racing back to Rían.

He swore under his breath as he hurried to catch up, pulling ghost tongue and devil's bittercress from his bag. But when he reached the corner, he came face-to-face with the glowing yellow eyes of a shifter.

"Naughty little mage. And here we thought you were a smart one."

Adrenaline spiking and heart pounding, Rían chucked the jars with a frantic command that caused both to immediately shatter. A haze of white powder and red bubbles exploded into the air, and he called on the wind as he exhaled to blow the mixture in the wolf's face. The man snarled as his skin blistered on contact.

Rían didn't linger. He threw himself around the toxic cloud and ran for the kitchen ahead.

"Niamh, where's the target?" He only had minutes before shifter healing combated his attack. What was a shifter even doing here? There'd been no mention of a bodyguard or hired gun. They were *supposed to tell him these things.*

Except they hadn't. Which meant this bastard was likely there to kill him on behalf of the Order. Fecking bastards.

Fine. This was fine. He could handle a shifter. Once he found the target and finished the mission, he'd either take out the shifter or disappear through a portal. Part of him wanted to open a portal then and there, but he wouldn't risk being labeled a deserter. He'd lose his freelance license and never find work anywhere again.

Niamh barked as she flew over the railing of the connected hallway and sailed down to the lower level.

Rían took one look over the edge, saw the glass table directly below, heard the shifter cursing from the kitchen, and threw himself over anyway. Another command word as he fell activated one of his amulets. A bright pure-silver bubble of light surrounded him, absorbing the impact as he crashed through the glass. Then he was racing after Niamh, to the top of a set of stairs in a narrow hallway leading down to yet another floor.

There was a loud crunch as the shifter landed in the shattered glass, and Rían swore. He grabbed a small jar full of a viscid black slime and threw it behind him as he started down the stairs. The jar shattered on impact, and the slime immediately spread across the floor, the top few stairs, and climbed up the entryway like a living web. It might not cause any damage, but at least shifter healing couldn't do anything about a slime stronger than epoxy.

Rían thundered down the stairs that ended at a solid iron door and hissed. He didn't have much fae blood, but he had enough that he could taste the iron in the air and fought the urge to sneeze. But iron was pervasive enough in the modern world that he knew how to deal with it.

From the top of the stairs came sudden disgusted cursing. "What the fuck is this shit?" the shifter howled.

Rían reached into his bag again, cursing this mission and the toll it was taking on his supplies as he pulled out a jar of blue-tinged silver liquid. Niamh chirped and swooped down to climb into her pouch with her brother, and Rían swiped a thumb over the triquetra amulet around his neck. Then he opened the jar and splashed the liquid on the door.

Absinthe of Winter, his own recipe, froze the door quickly enough that his breath frosted the air, but his amulet kept the sudden below-freezing temperature from affecting him. Another moment and the embrittled iron buckled and cracked.

The shifter snarled as he came into view, struggling down the stairs as the slime coating him kept sticking to the walls and steps. "Going to rip you apart, starting with your nails!"

Nope, nope, nope. He liked his nails right where they were.

Rían slammed his foot into the door, and it shattered as easily as the glass table. He shoved his hand into his bag again and rushed inside, eager to get this over with and leave before the shifter could make good on his threat. But the moment he crossed the threshold, he realized he'd walked from one trap right into another.

Manuel lay on the floor, his throat ripped out and his protruding belly slashed open.

Worse, the protective spells on all of Rían's amulets fizzled out beneath a nullifying barrier targeting his unique magic signature. Dread sank like a suffocating weight in his chest. Null fields were difficult to put together and more expensive than was usually worth the trouble. It was almost flattering that the Order went to so much trouble rather than set him free.

Instinct told him to run, but with the null field up he couldn't open a portal, and there was little chance of him getting back up the stairs. He took a slow step towards the nearest wall and glanced around. The space looked like some kind of panic room meets sex-torture dungeon. His skin crawled even as he deliberately refused to think about what a depraved man would have used it for.

Then his attention caught on the living shadows in the corner, before another shifter stepped out of them, and Rían's dread morphed into terror.

He really wished his ring for calm and clear thinking was working, because the last thing he wanted was to give the Mage Reaper any satisfaction of smelling the fear on him.

"Rían Fáidh," Reaper said. "I was hoping I would get the chance to add you to my collection."

"*Gabh suas*," Rían snarled, reflexively slipping into his mother tongue despite it not being as explicit as a succinct *Fuck you*. He pulled his aconite-coated dagger from his hip sheath. Even if he didn't have much of a chance to survive without his magic, he only needed to last a few minutes.

Reaper's aura was more black than silver, countless lines of violence and death running through it. "Ah ah ah, no need to be crude," he said, drawing closer with a casual air.

Rían would have gone for the stairs if the other shifter hadn't been nearing the bottom of them, still cursing and spitting threats. Instead he moved along the wall, farther into the room. He slipped in the blood spreading across the floor, his heart lurching at the thought that his own would soon be joining it.

Reaper chuckled as he stalked closer, drawing a slim dagger that glinted as dark as his aura. And then he moved, far faster than should have been possible, even for a shifter. Only shifters with mages bound to them could achieve those speeds.

Rían scrambled back, but he was no match for a shifter without his magic. His back hit the wall, his dagger knocked away with an expert twist, before a hand clamped around his throat.

"I'm going to take my time with you," Reaper said, his voice a sinister caress. His breath was hot on Rían's face, and it might have only been his imagination, but it smelled like cruelty and graves.

"*Buinneach dhearg ort*," Rían hissed, clawing at the hand around his throat. This couldn't be how he died, but wishing cancer on the bastard wasn't going to work quickly enough to save him. He kicked and twisted, but he went still when the point of the dagger pressed against the corner of his eye. His breath shuddered in his lungs, a scream building in his throat from fiery hot pain as Reaper slowly sliced the side of his face. He closed his throat rather than let the scream escape.

Another minute. Maybe two. So long as Reaper didn't slice an artery, Rían held out hope he could escape. His bag was full of volatile and questionably legal concoctions. All of them once securely sealed by the same magic that had fizzled out in his amulets. One in particular, a dual tube, one side filled with death nettle, the other with dragon sanguinary, was no longer separated by a spell.

"Whatever they're paying you I can double," Rían managed through gritted teeth.

Reaper laughed. "Taking you apart is half my payment." He glanced down when the pouch around Rían's neck shifted. He sliced through one of the straps, but Rían snagged the other before it could fall. He threw his shoulder into Reaper, ignoring the blade stabbing into his side as he ripped the pouch open with a harsh command to flee.

Both Niamh and her brother launched into the air, and Rían nearly choked on his relief when Niamh's wind magic still functioned. Only when they'd reached the exit and dodged the shifter stuck in the doorway did he turn his attention back to Reaper.

"Find them!" Reaper snarled at the other shifter before turning an amused look on Rían. "When I get my hands on them, I'm going to skin them alive."

Rían dropped his bag as he feigned defeat. The side facing him was burning red from intense heat, and an added kick to push it closer to Reaper ensured the ingredients mixed a bit faster. Even if he died in the resulting explosion, he could at least take the Order's pet assassin with him.

"You'll never lay a finger on them." He might die here, but he'd trained Niamh too well to get caught. She'd keep herself and her brother safe. If they'd been in the States, she may have even found her way to her sister and the pack who'd fucked up his plans for Denver.

Reaper looked about to say something else, before he apparently noticed the burning nettle smell. "The fuck did you do?" he snarled, reaching for the bag, but it was too late. The moment he opened the bag, the fresh air ignited the components, and an explosion ripped the house apart.

RÍAN WOKE to a flickering bubble of silver around him. His amulets, their magic restored, valiantly worked to protect him from an inferno.

Red-orange flames and black smoke surrounded him. A small pile of black ash was covered in bright blue flames, and he absently recognized it as a result of the Satan's jellyfish he'd added to his bag.

He coughed and pushed himself upright, ash and debris slipping off him and revealing the large shaft of wood sticking out of his thigh. He stared at it a moment, dull panic pounding beneath the headache making itself known.

When he tried to stand, his leg erupted in scream-inducing agony, and he was left panting and choking on the smoke wisping through his protective bubble. He had to get out of here, but there was no way he could climb the stairs to find an exit.

A warm breeze stirred the flames, and he twisted enough to see the entire back wall was gone, bits still crumbling off it. He glanced around in vain for his bag, but he knew it would have been obliterated. Years of work gone, but at least he was alive. He saw no sign of Reaper and snarled softly, unwilling to believe the shifter could have survived that, but he couldn't stick around to find out.

He crawled to the edge of the floor, his stomach swooping as he looked out at a very long drop.

"Niamh!" he called, coughing as his throat protested being used. His vision doubled and blackened at the edges as he struggled to stay conscious. If the Order had gone through all this trouble, he couldn't risk going to a healer, and his Sidhe didn't have any supplies that would keep him from dying. He'd gotten complacent, relying on the Order's top-notch healers for too long, and he hadn't anticipated being fatally injured and unable to access them.

Essentially, he was fucked.

He glanced up as Niamh glided down to him, her brother right behind. Once they were tucked safely into his shirt, he opened a doorway to the only option he feasibly had, no matter how badly he didn't want to.

When he'd set the wards for Lukas' pack, he'd added a backdoor for himself, just in case. He used that now, allowing himself to fall through the doorway he'd made and onto the living room floor of a shifter packhouse.

Lucky him, they were home.

There were a few shouts of alarm before he was surrounded by three shifters and their mage. "Sorry," he said, choking on his first breath of clean air. He was sure he was bleeding out all over their nice hardwood floors.

Max, the pack's promising new fire mage, dropped to his knees beside him, his expression pinched. "What the fuck? Who did this?"

Rían's bitter laugh cut off in a pained whine when Quinn, a shifter with red hair and Irish blood, ripped apart the fabric of his pants leg. Fierce swearing and sharp orders followed, but Rían couldn't focus on anything but the blinding pain as Quinn adjusted his leg.

He caught the single terrifying word of *hospital* and flailed his hand until he grabbed on to someone. "No," he said. "Order."

Lukas snarled from somewhere nearby. "They're not gonna touch you."

That might have been more reassuring if he knew he'd killed Reaper.

"There's no way we can get this out without causing damage," Quinn murmured.

Rían groaned, struggling to hold on to consciousness. If he passed out, he doubted he'd wake up again. "Burn it."

"No way," Max said. "You need an actual *doctor*."

"Burn it," he tried again, but he was fading fast.

Their words became a slurry of background noise, to the point he wasn't sure who was saying what anymore.

"You can do it, Max."

"This is insane."

"Bring all the supplies you can."

Everything went black, until a bright, blinding heat erupted in his leg, and he screamed. He fought briefly against the impossible weights holding him down, before he passed out completely.

CHAPTER 2

RÍAN HAD brief moments of clarity or impressions of his surroundings. Flurries of activity and frustrated words. Scorching heat, like he was in the middle of a desert. Moments when his nightmares and shadows came alive and tried to swallow him whole. Reaper's face, taunting him, carving him apart piece by piece, starting with his leg.

Finally the fever released its hold, and he woke to pale morning sunlight and Lukas slumped in a chair beside his bed. Even asleep the wolf looked terrible, with his mess of black hair and dark smudges under his eyes. He was propped up in an uncomfortable position against the nightstand, but he woke almost instantly when Rían tried to sit up.

Lukas blinked a few times before focusing on Rían with a wary frown. "If I give you a glass of water, are you going to try to smash it over my head again?"

He didn't remember doing that, but he managed a croaked "Probably."

Lukas shook his head with a snort and picked up a glass. "Glad to see you've regained your senses, squirrel."

Rían was far too parched for a witty comeback. He latched on to the glass and drank, spilling some in his desperate need for water. When it was empty, he handed it back, glad when some of the fog clouding his head faded. "How long?"

"About four days. It was touch and go for a while. You're lucky Caius' ex's fiancée is a trauma surgeon."

Rían scrubbed the grit out of his eyes before finally noticing the bandages wrapped around his arms.

"Burns," Lukas supplied when Rían stared at them in confusion.

He brushed his fingers over them with a soft grunt. The skin beneath felt tight and ached like a sunburn when he flexed his wrists. He blew out a slow breath and moved on, carefully tossing the covers back. He almost expected to find his leg missing, but it was there, wrapped up in a pound of gauze and white bandages. Even trying to activate the muscles sent sharp and dull aches through the entire limb, and he collapsed with a breathless groan.

If he'd had his bag, he could have fixed himself up in a few hours, but he had nothing. Not here anyway, but he wasn't quite willing to summon his Sidhe to see what all he had tucked away until he was more mobile. At least he'd transferred the entirety of his assets from the last eight years of working for the Order into a secure account not owned by them the moment he'd gotten his freelance license.

"If I give you a list of supplies, can you get them for me?"

Lukas raised an eyebrow before shaking his head with a soft huff. "Sure, I'll see what we can do."

Rían grimaced and gritted his teeth as he pushed himself into a proper sitting position, his stiff muscles protesting every twitch and flex. He looked across the room to the bathroom with a stifled groan. The distance may as well have been the entire Sahara Desert. He wasn't going to make it that far without magical aid, and his reserves were depleted.

Lukas stood and offered a hand, and as much as Rían hated to admit it, he needed the help.

Biting back a grumble, he grasped Lukas' wrist and let the wolf pull him to his feet, then leaned all his weight on Lukas as he hobbled to the bathroom. They passed the large cage in the corner, and he caught a brief glimpse of a pile of sugar gliders before Lukas maneuvered them through the bathroom door.

He grabbed the side of the counter for balance when they reached the toilet. When Lukas lingered, he managed a somewhat scathing look. "Gonna hold it for me?"

Lukas huffed and backed out of the bathroom, pulling the door shut behind him.

Rían took a moment when he was finally alone to close his eyes and breathe. He and the sugar gliders were still alive, he wasn't missing body parts, and he was technically free of the Order. Reaper would certainly come after him if—once—he learned Rían was still alive, but he wouldn't be taken by surprise again. He had the money to replace most of the supplies he'd lost, and the contacts for the harder-to-obtain ones. Everything could be replaced eventually, even if it took months.

His leg was a different story. Without a healer, he was stuck healing the mundane way, and that would take time and energy he didn't have to spare. The burns weren't as bad, though when he looked in the mirror he saw the full extent of the damage for himself. His hair had been singed into uneven patches, and someone had tried to clean away the soot and dirt to tend his face. Stitches were a dark line down the side of his cheek, and butterfly bandages took care of the spots closer to his eye. Dark bruises stained his throat in the shape of fingers, and more burns were scattered across his face and neck, as if burning debris had fallen on him before going out.

He looked away and breathed out the frustration and fear rather than let them take hold. Neither would help him right now. He took care of business as quickly as he could, and when he limped out of the bathroom, Lukas was waiting for him.

"Hungry?" he asked, and Rían made a face.

His stomach growled despite knowing the paltry food choices available here. "Anything but the grilled cheese."

Lukas laughed, and Rían was startled by how different it sounded from what he was used to. Not that he had heard the wolf laugh much, but he sounded happier. As Lukas half carried him down the stairs, Rían took a closer look at his aura. The connection from the binding Lukas had put on Max was still there, the bright pearlescence of a consensual binding. Beside it was the silvery twined mark of a fecking shifter claim.

No, two claims.

Fates above and below, what the feck was going on with this pack?

Lukas got him to the bottom of the stairs and carefully deposited him on the enormous sofa with his legs settled on the cushions.

Quinn was in the kitchen making what smelled like one of his weird grilled cheese sandwiches. He glanced over his shoulder with a grin. "Hey, you're finally off Death's door. You hungry?"

Rían stifled a whimper and glanced at Lukas, who looked far too amused. He narrowed his eyes as he noticed the dual claimings connected the two of them, on top of the bindings and claimings they both had with Max. He didn't see consensual bindings on mages often, certainly not within the Order, but he could see the power feedback loop they were creating here, and he was amazed that Max was still alive and sane.

"I think we have some apples," Lukas offered.

"Sure. Coffee?"

"How do you like it?" Quinn asked.

"Black." He rolled his eyes when Quinn made gagging noises in response.

Lukas brought back a large mug of coffee, a glass of water, and an apple to Rían, then sank into a chair and pulled out his phone. "What're the supplies you need?"

Rían had a list of a dozen of the more common items he needed, mage ivy first among them, as it was a staple for anyone skilled in alchemy, and he never kept surplus basics. The Order always had fresh components available, most grown in their greenhouses, but then he realized even his mortar and pestle were gone, along with all the jars and delicate tools he'd collected through the years.

His Sidhe still held his tomes, grimoires, and the rarer ingredients and items he'd gathered, and he still had the thirty-odd amulets and rings he always wore. Thankfully no one had removed them when tending his leg. He hadn't had much beyond that to begin with, but that bag had been the core of his life for the past decade, and it was gone because the Order didn't like to lose their hold on any mages. Especially not ones who'd excelled in every subject they'd offered.

"Squirrel?" Lukas asked.

Rían let out a humorless laugh because the alternative was to walk into the castle the Order called home and reduce it to rubble, which he was in no condition to do right then, even if he was pissed enough he thought he could pull it off. "Fine," he muttered. As unconvincing as that was, Lukas didn't press, merely typed out the ingredients Rían listed off.

By the time he'd finished his apple and coffee, he was in need of some serious painkillers, but he refused to touch modern pharmaceuticals. He preferred his own potions and their lack of serious side effects. He breathed through the pain as he found the small onyx orb on one of his necklaces and squeezed his hand around it. The relief was quick as the spells activated and deadened his sense of pain. That amulet had been useful more times than he liked to admit, considering he tended to skirt the edges of death when he had to use it.

He glanced up as Max came downstairs, a sugar glider on each shoulder and their albino brother on his head.

Rían raised an eyebrow. He couldn't exactly call it cute with the amount of raw power Max was radiating, but it came pretty close. He squinted against the bright aura, the swirl of oranges and reds with a hint of white and blue at his center. He'd thought it was bad when he first came here and saw the bindings of three shifters on the mage, but the three claims made it exponentially worse. Max's aura was bright enough to make Rían's eyes water, and he had to murmur a quick spell to put a magical blanket over Max to dim the intense glow.

Max settled on the other end of the sofa and tilted his head. "What was that?"

"A shield of sorts," he said, smiling faintly when Max stared at him in confusion. "You're very bright. It hurts my eyes."

"Oh, sorry."

Rían flicked his fingers. "Not your fault," he said with a pointed glare at Lukas. Then he noticed the way Quinn was leaning over the back of Lukas' chair and running a hand through his hair. That was new too. Even though he'd seen the dual claims between them, he'd assumed it was some kind of side effect from the claims they'd put on Max. But now that he was a bit more aware of his surroundings, the awkward yearning and pining he'd seen between them last time he was here was gone.

Even Max seemed far more settled and comfortable in his own skin, despite the few strands of gray Rían could see with the shield muting the overwhelming light of his aura. Not quite premeditated murders, but he'd been responsible for deaths recently. Not that Rían could judge, or was surprised, considering the Order couldn't take a hint unless it was bloody.

Caius came down the stairs a moment later, and it might have only been Rían's imagination that his black hair had a bit more silver in it than last time he was here. When he glanced at Max, his own aura flared brighter with affection and pride, and all of them were sparking with the pale reds of lust and desire, to the point Rían put a shield over all of them with a soft "Jesus fecking Christ" under his breath.

If he'd had his bag, he could have put on the glasses he'd spelled specifically to shut out other people's auras.

Caius poured himself a cup of coffee, then sat in the other oversized armchair. "So, should we be worried about the Order coming for us? Again," he asked dryly.

Rían couldn't help the faint twitch of his lips even if none of this was amusing. "Possibly," he said slowly. "I was on my last mission in Brazil. I made them give me my official discharge documents the morning before I left, so I'm technically free, but they sent their pet assassin after me. And I didn't see his corpse before I escaped. If he left me for dead, it might take them a while longer to realize I'm still alive."

He curled his fingers through the worn strip of red cloth tied around his wrist, surprised but relieved it had survived the fire. A charm another mage had given him shortly after he'd arrived at the Order. One meant to bring good luck and protection from evil. He should have let it wear down and fall off years ago, but he'd learned how to use stasis enchantments specifically to protect it. Even now he had a habit of rubbing the cloth between his fingers when he was stressed.

The Order wasn't likely to send anyone new after him, at least not right away, but Reaper wouldn't give up easily, especially if he really wanted Rían as part of his collection. He had no idea what that meant, but he could guess. He'd heard whispers through the years as others wondered if Rían's crimson eyes were the source of his abilities.

Most mages were lucky to find any talent in more than their main affinity. Thanks to his hint of fae blood, Rían's aptitude for magic let him dabble in just about everything with little effort. Grit, determination, and the knowledge that he needed every bit of power available to survive to a natural death of old age pushed him to hone every skill as far as he could, and his skills had earned him as many friends as it did envious rivals.

"If you can get me those supplies, I can be out of your hair by tonight," Rían offered. Even if he hadn't killed the bastard, he'd surely caused enough damage that even a shifter would need time to recover and track him down again, but the longer he stayed here, the more likely Caius and his pack would be drawn into the hunt.

Max frowned at him. "You can't leave like that. You can barely walk."

"I can patch myself up."

Lukas lifted his phone. "I'm not sure we can get all of this today."

Rían wrinkled his nose. As much as he despised the Order, he'd been spoiled with the ready availability of just about anything he wanted. "There's a shop I use when I'm in a pinch. They should have everything. And you may as well double the tools so Max can see if he has any talent for alchemy."

Max straightened, his aura sparking with eager excitement. "You'll teach me?"

"Briefly." Rían didn't like being indebted to anyone, and they'd saved his life. And anyway, he'd already planned to train Max once he was free, at least enough that he could protect himself from the Order. And anyone else who tried to get their hands on him.

CHAPTER 3

TOUA SWORE as he turned down another alley, pounding footsteps echoing behind him. The bastards were always chasing him, relentless and unforgiving enough to be one wrong move from finally catching up. No matter how hard he tried to keep off any magical radar or how many slums he passed through, they always caught up within a day or two.

For three months he'd been on the run. He knew they couldn't give up, and it didn't help that they had his magic signature and could find him anywhere in the world. His potion to stifle his magic was running low, and the length of time it lasted was getting shorter with every use. He couldn't keep relying on it, but he had no other options. He needed time to find supplies to make anything more efficient, and the last thing he wanted to do when he finally found a place safe enough to sleep for a few hours was spend his waning energy creating an amulet that might not even work. His talents were in healing, not the delicate spell-weaving required for personal protections.

Healing, and pissing off the California cartel.

Toua reached a main street and nearly crashed into a group of tourists, but he didn't have time to slow down. He spotted stairs leading down to the subway and took them three at a time, skipping the entire last set as he launched himself towards the platform.

He landed wrong, twisted his ankle as he fell, and rolled. He swiped the MetroCard he'd filched from some asshole yelling at a woman that morning as he hurried through the turnstile, then limp-ran the last few feet to throw himself onto the train a moment before the doors closed. He crashed into the other side with a gasping breath and turned in time to see the bastards who'd been chasing him through New York the past week and across the country for the past months.

He'd forgotten their names, if he ever learned them to begin with, so he'd dubbed them Tweedledum and Tweedledee. If not for their ability to track his magic, he was sure he'd have lost them shortly after running, even with their collared shifter tracking his scent. Caleb was only two steps behind the Tweedles, though he deliberately looked anywhere but at the train Toua had skidded into. The thick black choker around his neck served as a powerful shock collar that Toua had seen used more often than he liked in Caleb's single year under the cartel's thumb.

Tweedledee caught Toua's eye with a snarl as the train began to pull away, and Toua lifted two fingers to his temple in a mocking salute before they disappeared. Then he slumped to the sticky floor and hissed as he pressed his hand to his swelling ankle.

He didn't have much for an offering, but he called on his *zaj* spirit anyway, closing his eyes as he chanted under his breath. His dragon spirit answered readily enough, and warmth flared in his ankle before it faded, taking the pain and swelling with it. He had to be more careful. He was already toeing the line with how often he called on the spirits without the proper rituals in place. Much more and he ran the risk of being relegated to the spirit realm permanently.

Toua sagged against the wall in relief and exhaustion, pulling out the half-eaten protein bar he'd stolen yesterday and eating it in as many tiny bites as he could manage, leaving a piece of the corner for when he could make an offering. He had maybe a few hours before they tracked him down again, and he decided he needed to get out of the city. He was sick of the coasts. The oceans and their spirits were far too chaotic, and the press of eight million people around him was like drowning most days. He wanted mountains and trees.

Most of all he wanted to be able to stop running.

He didn't remember much of the Buddhist temple in Thailand where he'd grown up, and shortly after his family was granted asylum into the US, he'd Sparked. He'd already been training to become a shaman, and he remembered hoping that in the US he might be able to venture farther than specified walls, only for the Order to show up and steal him from his family.

Ten years stuck in that hellscape, and when he was released from service early it was to learn that his younger brother had gotten tangled up with a gang that crossed the cartel. Somehow he'd disappeared with half a million in drug money, and the Order, corrupt organization that they were, sold Toua to the cartel for another half million to work off both their debts.

He'd lasted nearly five years there. Long enough to ensure the rest of his family got out of the country and settled in France.

But healing gunshot wounds and stabbings for cartel thugs and keeping their leader—who liked his girls a little too young—from dying of his Stage 3 colon cancer was too much. He knew he'd never be free of them. Not until he died or ran. More than once he'd been tempted to poison them all. A few drops of death nettle oil in the soup and none of them would have woken in the morning.

But he was a healer.

A hungry, broke, exhausted healer.

He pulled out the nearly empty vial of potion that would throw off their tracking for a day or two if he was lucky and took a small sip. When the train finally stopped, he hurried out and found the nearest bus terminal, where he bought tickets to Texas, Colorado, and Washington with a stolen credit card. Then he shuffled the tickets, chose one at random, and waited twenty minutes before boarding the bus for Denver, Colorado.

It wasn't until he tucked himself into the seat at the very back that he noticed he'd stepped in something. He lifted his foot to find dog shit smeared across the bottom of his shoe. He hoped it was a dog's, anyway, and not a human's.

At least that was a sign that his luck was taking a turn for the better among his people, even if he was stuck with the smell for the next several hours.

With a groan he dropped his foot and slumped down a bit as he tried to get comfortable. He pulled the remaining tiny piece of protein bar from his pocket and pulled down the small tray on the back of the seat in front of him. It was a far cry from a real table, much less a proper altar, but he dropped the granola piece in the tiny circle cup holder as he offered it to his dragon spirit in thanks for the healing.

When the bus began moving a short time later, he propped his head against the window to try and get some sleep. He had two days to rest.

Then he'd have to find someone who could make more of his potion before he started the cycle all over again.

CHAPTER 4

IT TURNED out that Max did have a knack for alchemy, especially after Rían likened it to art rather than cooking. Recipes existed for a reason, but most of them were flexible. Too many components played into determining the final product to follow a recipe exactly: the quality of ingredients, whether they were fresh or dried, the weather, the caster's mood, or how much raw magic was poured into the product.

Once Rían was able to patch up his leg well enough to limp without more than a twinge of pain, he spent an entire afternoon teaching Max how each element would affect his potions. "After every second or third ingredient, you want to make sure its energy and color matches the recipe and adjust until it does."

"Did you just say I need to vibe check my potions?"

Rían tipped his head back with a groan as Max laughed. He was sure this was part of why the Order insisted on training mages as young as possible. Not only was it easier to control a bunch of scared kids when they didn't have parents around to run to, it was easier to homogenize them. Not just with standardizing their lessons, but erasing their first language and culture, until their sole identity was mage and their only loyalty was to the Order.

And it worked on most. At least until they turned sixteen and were finally allowed back into the real world. They may have been assigned a mentor for the first several months, to ensure they knew they couldn't run, but the Order couldn't watch every mage for every moment, and the majority of them weren't psychopaths. They could see for themselves that some of their missions were shady. Kids learned the difference between right and wrong, or fair and unfair, years before the Order started brainwashing them.

Rían had fought hard to hold on to his Irish accent and language, listening to Irish music or audiobooks whenever he could, but he still felt like an impostor whenever he was too tired to make the effort to keep his accent. It shouldn't have *required* effort.

"Uhh, red is bad, right?" Max asked.

Rían jerked back to the present in time to see the smoking crucible and the bright red liquid bubbling inside. He threw himself over the table, ignoring the sharp pain of protest in his leg as he tackled Max to the ground and activated two of his protective amulets.

Max yelped but didn't struggle, though when nothing happened for a long moment, he squirmed. "Was that really necess—"

A loud bang like a rifle firing over their heads reverberated through them. Shards of melting porcelain bounced off the protective shield surrounding them, landed on the floor where they turned the hardwood black, or embedded into the walls. There was an ominous cracking sound, and Rían looked up to see a spiderweb spreading across the back sliding glass door.

Footsteps thundered on both sets of stairs and from down the hall as three pissed-off shifters with guns drawn stormed into the room.

"What the fuck?" Caius demanded, moving straight for Max as Quinn and Lukas checked for threats.

"My fault," Rían said, rolling off Max and out of Caius' way.

"It was not," Max snapped, leaning into Caius and patting the wolf's chest. "I fucked up a potion and it exploded."

Rían picked himself up, wincing when he put pressure on his leg and found he'd likely reversed what patchwork he'd done on it. He eyed the still smoldering globs of what was essentially lava before grabbing the bit of winter's breath they'd managed to find. He picked off the soft white flowers and rubbed them between his hands, infusing them with a bit of wind and water magic before sprinkling them over the mess.

The heat vanished beneath the freezing ability of the flowers, reducing the lava to inert black gunk. Then he limp-hopped to the nearest chair and sank into it. "I'll fix it in a sec."

Caius raised an eyebrow as he glanced at the door and bits of porcelain stuck in the walls. There was even a sizable shard sticking out of the fridge. "All of it?" he asked dubiously.

Any other time Rían would have been offended, but he'd forgotten how utterly exhausting it was to heal without the aid of magic. One of the only upsides to the Order: free instant healing. He wiggled his fingers at Caius. "Magic."

"Can you show me how to fix it?" Max asked, picking at the largest glob of gunk on the table, but it had melted a good quarter of an inch into the wood.

Rían smiled faintly. "Fire magic is destructive by nature."

Max pouted before taking in the extent of the damage with a wince. "You can really fix all this?"

"Your lack of faith is disturbing," he replied dryly, earning a snicker from both Lukas and Quinn. He closed his eyes and breathed as he reached for his source of magic. He usually preferred using his magic for wards or amulets, relying on his bag to do the heavy lifting for most spells, but something like this tapped into the true essence of his magic—spatial manipulation.

He focused on the crucible, on the cold earth and clay that was scattered in pieces around the room. When he latched on to its unique magical signature, he urged the pieces to call to each other and opened his eyes to guide them all back to the table without causing more damage. Once they were all in place, he suggested they reform themselves to how they'd been before the explosion. Each piece realigned and resealed itself to its neighbors, until the entire crucible was as good as new. Then he did the same for the glass door and the fridge, before slumping against the table.

"I'll finish the rest tomorrow," he said, reaching for one of the tonics he'd made while showing Max the basics. He drained it and breathed through the burn until it settled in his gut and replenished some of the energy he'd used. He blinked as a glass of water appeared in front of him and glanced up at Quinn with a murmured thanks before drinking.

Max dropped into the chair next to Rían with a wistful sigh. "I wish I could do that."

"Fire suits you better," Quinn replied, reaching over to muss Max's hair and smirking in the face of his glare.

"Thank you," Caius said.

Rían waved him off, pulling his new phone out when it chimed with a text. The crew he'd hired was done with his shop, and he needed to verify there were no issues and sign off on their work. He made a face as he considered how safe it could be. It needed wards, and if the Order knew or suspected that he was still alive, they'd be able to find out he'd leased the property.

"What's wrong?" Lukas asked.

"My shop is done."

"Your tattoo shop?" Max sat up with far too much interest. "Can I come?"

Rían hesitated and glanced at Caius. The last thing he needed was a shifter pack hunting his ass if Max got hurt because of him.

Caius raised an eyebrow. "You're worried about the Order."

"Until I can get it properly warded, yes." He didn't have the energy for that today, not when he needed to patch up his leg again. Unfortunately, his magic didn't work on living organic matter.

"We could all go," Quinn suggested.

As much as he appreciated the thought and the potential strength in numbers, they weren't his pack, and he didn't want them getting involved in another power play with the Order because of him.

"You'll be safer if we all go," Caius said.

"You won't be," Rían replied, meeting Caius' storm-gray eyes.

Caius almost looked amused, and the brief flare of pale yellow in his aura confirmed it. "Since I appear not to have a choice about stepping into the power vacuum we created, I don't think the Order is our main concern right now."

Rían raised an eyebrow and looked between them in confusion. "What power vacuum?"

CHAPTER 5

RÍAN DRAINED the third beer someone had given him at some point before burying his face in his hands. He'd thought the loss of his precious dead zone was the worst he'd have to deal with, but apparently Caius and his pack were hell-bent on making his life as miserable as the Order had.

"What do you *mean* you're taking the place of the Italian mafia?" He didn't whine, on account of the fact that he was a powerful mage and whining was beneath him, but he was a little drunk because not only had his family abandoned him, but so had any genetic alcohol tolerance. "There's only four of you. What the feck do you expect to do other than die bloody?"

"Gee, tell us how you really feel," Lukas muttered.

Rían dropped his hands and glared at the wolf, but before he could tell him off, Max piped up.

"My father didn't explicitly write me out of his will. Or specify what he wanted done in case my sister vanished. Most of the paperwork is already done. We're just waiting on licensing and permits for the casino before I inherit everything in her place."

Rían turned his head to stare at Max. He'd expected some kind of distress over dead or missing family members, but Max's aura was mostly calm. Considering his father had tried to kill him, that was understandable, but "Your sister vanished?"

Max shrugged with a brief flare of guilt, but it faded quickly. "We filed a missing person's report, but she was taken by Ghost."

The name made him wince. He'd met Ghost a few times when he'd worked with the military, and he hoped to never see her again. "And you're okay with that?"

"She drugged me and handed me over to a shifter who forced a binding on me." He sounded angry, but his aura belied his hurt.

Rían winced and rubbed his eyes. He should have listened to his gut and given up on his plans to settle here. The Order and their pet assassin were one thing, but a citywide war for power was the last thing he wanted involved in. He'd be too tempted to destroy the rest of the competition to ensure the violence didn't spill onto the streets. "You're all insane," he muttered.

"Yeah, isn't it great?" Quinn said with a laugh. "I haven't had this much fun since demolition training."

He muttered a plea for help to whatever old gods might still be listening, though that was likely only inviting more trouble. He didn't want any part of this. Except in his drunken state, he thought he could see how he could ensure they could all get exactly what they wanted.

The Order was already wary of Max and silently seething that Caius' armed forces connections meant the government was keenly aware of the situation here. Maybe they could have amassed their forces and taken Caius' pack and Max out before, but now that Rían was free, the Order had lost one of their most powerful mages. The second in nearly as many months, considering Max's little stunt of burning the Order's bindings off the last mage they'd sent after him.

"Do you even have a plan?" Rían asked.

Caius' lips twitched in bemusement. "Being a decorated colonel didn't exactly prepare me for taking over a city's underworld."

"You can't tell me you convinced your father's men to swear loyalty to you."

Max snorted. "I didn't have to. I'm a mage, and even if I was never meant to inherit, I know all their secrets. And I know how the businesses work."

"Didn't hurt that the few who decided to speak out quietly disappeared," Lukas added, clinking his bottle against Quinn's with a smug smirk.

Scratch that. They weren't insane. They were morally compromised and homicidal, but who wasn't these days.

But that wouldn't be enough, he knew. Even if the bindings and claims they'd put on Max were making them far more powerful than most shifters, there were still only three of them. And while Max had enough raw power to reduce the entire city to ash with the force of a nuclear bomb, he was completely untrained.

Rían slumped against the table with a groan. He wasn't getting involved. He wasn't. He'd cancel the lease on his shop and find somewhere new where he could disappear.

He might owe them for saving his life, but he didn't owe them *his life*.

And they had no idea what they were doing. Best case scenario, they'd hold out for a year, maybe two, before someone more ruthless decided to come after them. Likely someone contracted by the Order, especially if they wanted a foothold here to snatch up the mages that would certainly be Sparking soon. He hadn't sensed any since he'd arrived, certainly not like he'd first sensed Max, but maybe the magic was still settling. Or the only three shifters in the area all being bound to a mage already meant the balance was stable. If that was the case, unless more shifters joined the pack or started their own, there wouldn't be new mages Sparking here for a while.

As much of a relief as that was, a tiny shifter pack had no chance of surviving here.

"Wow, you're really giving off all the 'I'm doomed' scents," Quinn said dryly.

Rían raised his middle finger without lifting his face from the table. He groaned again and finally pushed himself up. "I'm going to bed." Except he doubted he'd get much sleep with the way his thoughts were buzzing.

He limped his way up the stairs and face-planted on the bed with another groan. Fourteen years he'd been waiting and planning for his freedom. The fact the Order had never been able to put a binding on him was one of the only things that got him through the last few years, but he also wasn't stupid enough to think they'd let him get away so easily.

He may not have much fae blood, but he apparently had enough to keep a binding he didn't want from sticking and to summon his own personal Sidhe. Maybe he could crawl inside it and hide for a few years. Fates knew he could use a break.

But he liked a challenge. Mastering all the so-called courses the Order offered had been the only thing to keep him sane when he was younger, and using the contraband books and materials his grandmother managed to sneak to him ensured he never fell into the narrow-minded thinking the Order loved to promote.

He flopped onto his back and stared at the ceiling but quickly closed his eyes when he swore he saw it moving. He shouldn't have had that third beer, but he'd needed it to deal with the sheer amount of stupidity downstairs. And his own stupidity for thinking three shifters and an untrained mage would offer any kind of chance of helping him make a stand against the Order.

What little amount of live-and-let-live apathy they'd scored with him had burned down with that house in Brazil. He couldn't take them down alone, and he didn't want to destroy them completely until another magic authority could take their place in training new mages or the ruling council could be replaced, but he did want to make sure they left him and his city of choice the fuck alone.

He let out a soft hum as he let the fantasy run wild. As much as he hated shifters on the principle of binding mages whenever they got the chance, it wasn't like other mages were any better. If mere humans ever figured out how to claim mages for themselves, Rían had no doubt they'd be even worse.

The question was, were they willing to help him, and was he willing to do the one thing he swore he'd never do: become part of a pack?

CHAPTER 6

RÍAN SPENT the early morning creating a temporary link between his Sidhe and the en suite bathroom, then gathering and sorting through the boxes of supplies he'd been putting together the last two years in anticipation of opening his shop. Everything from a dozen colors of tattoo ink, bottles of various potions—minor protection, restful sleep, calming energy—and a handful of amulets he'd made in his spare time with similar enchantments were all neatly tucked away. He'd even found a few viable healing tonics to take the edge of pain off his face and leg, and an old burn ointment that smelled like rotting crayons when he opened it.

The ointment he tossed in the trash; then he retrieved his laptop bag and one of the many crystals he had stored among his extra components. He set an alarm trigger in the crystal and infused it with enough latent energy to last for a year.

He found the gauze and bandages by the bed and covered the stitches in his face as best he could, which was poorly, but he was more upset about his hair than his injuries. Eventually he'd be able to patch himself up, but his hair couldn't be fixed with some potions or spells. He'd have to wait for it to grow out.

Having three shifters on hand meant the supplies got loaded into the back of their SUV within minutes, and that afternoon found all five of them, along with their sugar glider familiars safe in their pouches, in his tattoo shop. The smells of fresh paint and new leather from the sofa and tattoo chairs were heavy in the air.

Rían grabbed the crystal and found the center of the shop, then opened a hole with a twist of magic, deep enough to sit right below the warding set in the foundation. He dropped the crystal in, wrapped it in its own tight warding on all sides except the top touching the shop's wards, and resealed the hole. Once he had his own wards properly in place, the alarm would trigger if anyone tampered with or breached his security.

He was still disturbed by how easily Reaper had rendered him powerless. Relying on his bag and magic to always be there in any situation had become a crutch, and he was sure his ancestors were rolling in their graves knowing he'd never learned to properly throw a punch. Not that someone like Reaper could be taken out with a fist. Maybe he should carry more than an aconite-coated dagger for a while.

Rían pushed those thoughts away and turned to walk Max through the basics of how to set a ward. How to feel the edge of the domain he wanted to shield and how to attach magic along that edge. All the while he was acutely aware of the three wolves sprawled out on his new leather sofa and a tattoo chair.

Max handled wards a bit better than his last potion, and they had the simplest of protections in place within half an hour. Rían sank onto the leather stool behind the bare counter to give his leg a rest. Max leaned over the counter with his arms crossed on the other side. "So I don't see a logo on your window."

Rían raised an eyebrow at the flare of enthusiasm in Max's aura and glanced at his shop window. The only things on it were his shop name—Inkindle—and a small symbol in the lower right-hand corner of a stylized eye with a line through it. The symbol might not mean much to the general public, but it was a sign to other mages that the shop was run by a licensed mage not bound to the Order. "I don't have one. Why?"

Max grinned and pulled his phone out of his back pocket. He tapped the screen a few times before turning it to face Rían. "How do you like this?"

On the screen was a triquetra made of flames. It was surprisingly fitting, and he was sure Max had used his own flames as inspiration. Natural and magical flames might look alike, but where natural fires were a gradient of color or turned black at the edges, magical flames tended to remain a solid color that depended on the heat and power poured into them. "You just happened to have made this."

Max shrugged. "I might have been designing it since you mentioned setting up shop here."

"I like it," Rían said. "And I have most of what's needed for a spell to put it up."

"There's a components shop not far from here," Max said before Rían could suggest getting the rest of the supplies later. "Is it a spell you can teach me?"

"Sure," he said, unsurprised by the eagerness to learn. Max might have Sparked later in life than the vast majority of mages, but one thing among them was universal: Every mage held a desire to learn and test the limits of their skills. At least until the Order got hold of them.

Max grinned and straightened, bouncing on his feet. "What do we need? We'll go get it."

"Oh, we will, will we?" Lukas called, proving they'd been eavesdropping. Not that the shop was large enough for much expectation of privacy, even without shifter hearing.

"I can order the rest later," Rían said. He needed to get a new bag to start rebuilding his everyday supplies soon anyway. Now that he'd retrieved his laptop, he needed to resume his search for a place to live, though he was leaning heavily towards using his Sidhe; he was fairly certain the Order couldn't track its fae magic.

"No, we can get it," Max insisted. "I've never been inside one, and I have access to my own money now."

"In other words, you plan to buy one of everything?" Rían asked, shaking his head when Max offered an unrepentant smirk. "We'll need more mage ivy," he said, trying to remember what all he'd seen in his Sidhe. "Grax if they have it. Viscid dogbane if they don't."

Max squinted at him. "You're making those up."

Rían snorted. "I wish. Even if you don't want to learn alchemy, you'll still have to memorize most of the plants and components used for the more complicated spells."

With a groan Max pushed away from the counter. "Is that all you need?"

"I'll have to check and text you if I'm missing anything else."

Max turned and wiggled his fingers at the others. "Come, my minions."

Caius and Lukas gave exasperated sighs, but Quinn laughed as he stalked forward, picked Max up, and tossed him over a shoulder in a fireman's carry. "If I'm a minion I expect more perks," he said, slapping Max's ass on his way out the door.

Rían rolled his eyes and blew out a breath when the door closed behind them and he was finally, blissfully alone. He scrubbed a hand over his face and enjoyed the silence for a long moment, then stood and started picking items out of the boxes in the corner. His leg was starting to ache again, but he powered through it as he limped back and forth across the shop.

The door chimed as he was arranging the tattoo inks, and he turned in surprise, sure they couldn't have found the supplies and returned so quickly, but it wasn't them. A mage stood in the open doorway, his aura dim from both physical and magical exhaustion.

The words *We're not open* died in Rían's throat as he took a hesitant step forward. "Can I help you?"

The mage shuddered and let the door close behind him. "I hope so." His voice was rough, and there was an almost defeated air to him. "I need a potion made," he said, pulling a worn scrap of paper from his pocket.

Rían took it as he approached and moved around the counter to sit on his stool. One look at the ingredients and he nearly recoiled, his lips twisting in distaste as he did the calculations of the amounts scribbled to the side. "This is essentially poison," he said tightly, glancing at the man's aura again. A poison to diminish someone's magical signature, to make it harder to track. The Order liked for their mages to use it when sending them into countries where they wanted to avoid drawing attention to themselves, but it wasn't meant to be used more than once or twice at a time.

From what he could see, the mage had been using it for months. "There are better options if you're on the run from the Order," he said.

"It's not the Order I'm hiding from."

Rían tilted his head. Something about the aura and voice were familiar, and he focused on the mage directly. Worn and frayed clothes, the distinct odor of someone who hadn't bathed in weeks, if not months. Dark hair and eyes, and East Asian characteristics. He followed the mage's gaze to his wrist and the strip of red cloth tied around it, and his breath stuck in his throat. "Toua?"

Toua's lips tugged into a hesitant smile. "You remember me?"

"Why wouldn't I?" Not everyone in the Order had been a nightmare to deal with, but Toua was one of the few who'd been genuinely kind. He eyed the paper again with a frown. "And why do you need this? Why not use an amulet?"

Toua shifted on his feet. "The kind I need is a bit beyond my abilities at the moment."

Rían pulled one of his rings off without thinking. It was one of his older ones, and he was likely being stupid since he couldn't know whether the Order still suspected he was alive, but he knew beyond a doubt that Toua needed it more than he did. Even if he had the ingredients for the potion, there wasn't a chance in hell he would make it for someone in danger of destroying their magical essence.

Besides, Caius' packhouse was warded well enough to protect him until he could replace the ring and get his shop warded the same.

"I can't take this," Toua said, staring at the ring sitting on his palm like it was a snake poised to strike. "Even if it wasn't yours, I can't afford it."

"Then take it as a gift."

"That's no way to do business."

Rían narrowed his eyes. If he didn't know better, he might have sworn Toua was laughing at him.

Then again, he didn't know better. The last time he'd seen Toua was several years ago, shortly before he'd finished his time with the Order. As a spirit healer, the Order had never been able to place a proper binding on him. There weren't many of them, not compared to all the other types of healers and mages, and healers were lucky enough to be in demand in the mundane world that the Order couldn't quietly dispose of them like they'd tried with Rían.

Toua relented in the face of Rían's glare and slipped the ring on. Once it was in place, Rían pressed a fingertip to the silver and attuned the anti-scrying and signature-blocking spells to Toua's magic.

"There," he murmured. "Whoever's tracking your magic won't be able to find you now."

Toua let out a shuddering breath and nearly sagged in relief. "How long will it last without recharging?"

"A week or two, even if they're persistent. Long enough for me to make one specifically for you." He wasn't sure why he offered, except Toua had given him a charm of protection that helped him feel safe enough to become the mage he was, and this felt like a chance to repay that gift. And he could admit that he'd hated when Toua disappeared, and he wanted an excuse to see him again.

Toua stared at him in disbelief. "If I can't afford one, I certainly can't afford a second."

Rían shrugged. "I'm sure I have a suitable ring somewhere." Amulet-grade jewelry wasn't cheap, but most of his supplies he'd pilfered from the Order, so he didn't consider it a loss.

"Still…." He glanced from Rían's face to his leg and cleared his throat. "I could heal that, if you'd like. It's not much, but—"

"More than enough," Rían said quickly, hating how desperate he was for magical healing. Being in pain *sucked*. He didn't see any of Toua's usual supplies, which wasn't surprising, if he was on the run, and he didn't remember what they were; most of what little time they spent together had been stolen moments of freedom in the library. "Do you need anything to do it?"

Toua shook his head but then said, "Incense?"

"I might have some. Let me check." He pushed to his feet and headed to the small supply room, ensuring the door was shut before calling his Sidhe to appear on the other side and stepping through. He never had much use for the spirit paper or incense shamans used, but he wasn't ashamed to admit he'd developed klepto tendencies whenever he saw supplies left unattended, especially in the Order's storerooms.

What little guilt he may have felt over it had burned up with his bag of supplies.

He was still pissed about his bag, more than the actual attempt on his life, and he would likely die mad about it.

CHAPTER 7

TOUA TILTED his head as he felt an unfamiliar pulse of energy before Rían disappeared through a door, then glanced down at himself with a grimace. When he'd seen the symbol in the corner of the window, he'd known this was where he was meant to be, where he would have a chance to turn his luck around, but finding Rían here was the last thing he'd expected.

He almost hadn't recognized Rían, except his eyes were unmistakable. A striking, unique shade of red that hinted at something more than human in his bloodline, but he couldn't fathom what. Outside of shifters, most other creatures were the stuff of legends and myths.

Then there was the red protection string tied around Rían's wrist. It certainly wasn't Toua's best work, even when he'd been under the Order's watch he rarely had time to make proper *khi tes*, but he'd poured all the energy he could to ward off evil and protect Rían from whatever horrors came his way. The fact Rían still wore it was as surprising as the fact it was still in good condition. The protective spells were faded, but he was touched that Rían had kept it rather than throw it in the trash as subpar compared to a "proper" amulet. He even still wore it on his wrist.

And now here Toua was, rancid from months without anything more than gas station sinks to wash himself and looking like the transient he technically was. He tensed as the shop door opened behind him and glanced over his shoulder.

"They didn't have any grax," a young man called, and the strength of magical power around him was almost stifling. The mage and the three men behind him all stopped in the doorway, clustered together and inconveniently blocking any chance of escape. "Hi," the mage said. "Where's Rían?"

"Looking for some incense," Toua replied, eyeing the other three as his instincts urged him to keep still and make no sudden moves. Something that usually only happened near shifters.

The mage hummed before stepping closer and offering his hand. "What's he need incense for? I'm Max, by the way."

Toua couldn't stifle his surprise and hesitantly shook, glad he'd at least found a restroom that morning so his hands were relatively clean. "Toua. And it's something I use for some spells."

Max grinned and moved to set a large box and several bags behind the counter, which seemed to be the signal for the others to move away from the door and drop their own boxes there. "What kind of mage are you?" Max asked, propping his elbows on the counter.

He didn't miss the blatant protective positioning of two of the men while the black-haired one moved to the wall behind Toua and leaned back with his arms crossed. "Spirit healer," he replied, distracted by his anxiety ramping up at being boxed in. As much as he wanted to repay Rían for the amulet, he wasn't sure his nerves could take this much longer.

"The feck are you gobshites doing?" Rían snapped, slamming the door behind him and managing to stalk across the room despite the obvious limp.

Toua raised his eyebrows in surprise, sure that wasn't the sweet, lost kid he'd met over a decade ago.

The redhead lifted his hands in surrender and quickly moved to sprawl on the couch.

Rían narrowed his eyes and glowered at each of them until the other two also moved to the other side of the shop, but Max seemed unfazed, only stepping aside enough to let Rían sit on the stool.

"What's a spirit healer? Is that like metaphysics?" Max asked, yelping when Rían kicked his leg. "Ow! What did I do?"

Toua coughed a laugh. "Most mages don't like being questioned about their powers."

"Why not?"

"Because if the Order ever wants you dead, they'll use all the information they can to send someone who has an advantage over you," Rían said, bitter anger in his words.

Max frowned. "Is that why they sent that water mage after me?"

"Most likely," Rían said before turning to Toua and handing over a few sticks of incense. "Is this enough?"

Toua took them with a faint smile of relief. They weren't strictly necessary since he had no other supplies or altar, but it'd been months since he'd touched anything close to his tools. "Yes, thank you." He pulled out his lighter, but he'd used the last of the fluid to start a dumpster fire for warmth a week ago, and it refused to light.

Max held a finger out, a small orange flame flickering at the end of it. A fire mage. That would explain some of the amount of power he sensed coming off him.

"Thanks," he said, lighting one of the sticks and closing his eyes as he whispered a chant thanking his dragon spirit for its help and asking for its continued guidance. Then he set it carefully on the edge of the counter and turned his attention to Rían. "I'll need to see the damage."

A light flush spread across Rían's cheeks. "It's my thigh."

Toua nodded. "I can work over your clothes, but it would be far more effective if I can touch near the wound." He ignored the distinct tingling on the back of his neck, sure at least one of the shifters was plotting to rip his heart out, and kept his eyes on Rían.

"Fine," he grumbled, standing and dropping his pants to his knees without preamble. Then he sank onto the stool again and worked the bandage off his leg.

Toua stepped around the counter, catching a glimpse of boxers with smiley faces on them before forcing his attention to the injury with a wince. That looked gnarly, and far more worrying than he'd expected from what little he'd sensed, thanks to the potion he'd been taking. Half of Rían's thigh was bruised nearly black, with a large wound on either side, mostly scabbed over and too big for stitches. What he'd thought would be a quick and easy heal was most decidedly not going to be quick or easy. As distressing as the bruises, burns, and whatever was hiding under the shoddy bandage on Rían's face were, the severity of his leg was worse.

"I can't heal that all in one go," Toua said. His magic was far too depleted from the potion and exhaustion.

"Anything is better than this," Rían said.

With a nod, Toua picked up another stick of incense and hoped two would be enough to take the brunt of the energy drain. "If you would be so kind," he said, holding the stick out to Max, who offered his flame again.

Toua lit the incense, then pressed the fingers of his other hand into five separate points as far around Rían's leg as he could. He closed his eyes, breathing in the scent of smoke and flame and spicy, woody scent of the incense as he let himself fall into a trance. He called on his dragon spirit to heal Rían's leg. To mend the skin and muscle. To cleanse the infection threatening to take hold.

Flesh warmed beneath his fingers as he poured some of his magic into it to aid his spirit, but it wasn't enough. Not nearly enough to do more than ease the pain and nudge the healing along so it was closer to two weeks healed rather than a few days.

Toua released his magic and slumped against the counter, fighting a wave of nausea as vertigo swept over him. Maybe he'd used too much magic, considering he hadn't eaten anything since finishing the last of his protein bar on the bus. But it felt good to heal someone who actually deserved it for once.

"Sit down," Rían ordered, guiding him to the stool, and Toua didn't have the strength to protest. "I know one of you has food on you."

"Here," someone said.

Toua cracked his eyes open to see the redhead toss a candy bar over on his way to the door.

"More sugar?" the shifter asked.

"And protein," Rían said, ripping the candy open and shoving it in Toua's face with a glower. The fierce expression was one he remembered well enough that he chuckled as he took a bite. "If I'd realized you were that depleted, I wouldn't have let you heal me."

"Let me?" Toua replied, raising an eyebrow. "I seem to recall having seniority."

Rían narrowed his eyes, opening his mouth for what was certain to be a scathing remark, but the younger shifter on the couch cleared his throat.

"Might wanna pull your pants up, squirrel."

Rían hissed, a flush staining his cheeks again as he shimmied his pants back into place. "Feck off, wolf," he snarled.

Max hummed from beside Toua. "You're not with the Order, then?"

"No. I haven't been under their thumb for about five years now."

"You don't look thirty."

Toua chuckled. "Thank you?"

Rían crossed his arms as he propped a hip against the counter. "Why don't you tell me who you're running from?"

He finished the candy with a rueful twist of his lips. "I'm not a mission."

"You implying I can't help?" Rían demanded, narrowing his eyes.

Toua lifted his hands in surrender. "I'm suggesting you don't need to get involved."

"Why not?" Max asked. "Not like it can be any worse than the Order or the mafia."

Toua winced and felt four intense gazes zero in on him.

"Which one?" Rían demanded.

He tipped his head back with a groan, but honestly, he was so tired of running that the thought of Rían helping despite apparently being fresh out of the Order's grasp was enough that he sagged in defeat. "West coast. The drug cartel out near Fresno."

"Sounds fun. Do you know them?" Max asked.

Toua wasn't sure who he was talking to until the older shifter with the lingering damage of an old injury in his shoulder gave Max a pained look. His aura was weak enough he could barely even sense anything, but it was still surprising to sense anything on a shifter. Aconite-infused weapons were the only thing that could do that kind of damage, and he nearly winced in sympathy. "I'm starting to think the image you have of me is beyond repair."

Max snorted. "You could have just said no."

The door opened, and the shifter who'd left returned with two bags stuffed full of food and drink from a convenience store, which he proceeded to set out on the counter.

Toua stared at it all in confusion until Rían picked up two hotdogs and the packs of mustard, ketchup, and relish and shoved them in Toua's hands. "Eat." Then Rían grabbed a hotdog for himself, covered it in mustard, and ate half in one bite.

"Sexy," the shifter said with a waggle of his eyebrows and laughed when Rían flipped him the finger. He turned to Toua and held his hand out. "I'm Quinn. The grumpy Daddy is Caius. And the one with a ten-foot pole stuck up his ass is Lukas."

Toua spared a quick look at Rían when he choked before dropping his hotdog and condiments to shake the offered hand, sparing a quick glance at the couch for the others' reactions to Quinn's descriptions, but they seemed more resigned than anything.

Quinn pulled out a can of Dr Pepper and popped the tab. "Please tell me you like to drink this. I'm sick of being surrounded by heathens," he said, holding the can out.

Toua was far too overwhelmed and hungry to turn down a half-eaten sandwich off the street, much less a crisp, cold, untouched soda. He took the can and drank, closing his eyes with a soft moan and draining the entire thing in one go. Which was a mistake because a moment later he let out a belch that seemed to last forever.

Quinn cackled. "I'd give that an eight," he said, pulling out another can and heading to the sofa with it, where he sat in Lukas' lap. "What'd I miss?"

"We're taking down a drug cartel," Max said, rummaging through the bag and snatching a pack of chips.

Caius tipped his head back with a fervent "Fenrir help me."

Lukas snorted. "You keep asking for help. I don't think he's listening anymore."

Toua popped the hotdog containers open. "You really don't need to get involved." He didn't want to be responsible for anyone getting caught or injured in the crossfire whenever the cartel inevitably caught up to him again. Even with Rían's ring, the potion had worn off shortly after arriving in the city. There was a good chance they already knew he was here and could pick up his scent.

"No offense, but you look like shit," Rían said. "How long have you been on the run?"

"A few months," he said, adding the ketchup, mustard, and relish to one of his hotdogs. Not for the taste but for the calories, even if they were mostly empty chemicals.

"Do you have a place to stay?" Caius asked.

Toua froze, unsure how he should answer. He'd already gotten far more than he ever expected to from stepping into this shop. He took a large bite to buy himself some time.

Rían crossed his arms again. "I'll know if you're lying."

That sounded like a challenge, and he licked his lips after swallowing. "My arrangements are suitable to my needs."

Crimson eyes narrowed as Rían bent forward until they were almost nose to nose. "Do your *arrangements* include a shower and a bed?" he asked like it was a threat.

Toua swallowed against the strange twist of warmth in his gut, something he hadn't felt… ever. "No," he admitted without meaning to.

Across the room, one of the shifters snorted. "I suppose I can give up my bed to the squirrel."

"Oh, are you volunteering to sleep on the sofa?" Quinn asked. "How kind of y-ow!" He doubled over with a laugh. "Now you're gonna have to beg to share my bed."

Toua glanced at them in bewilderment. "That's not—"

"Toua."

He snapped his mouth shut and slanted a wary glance at Rían from the corner of his eye.

"Eat the food and stop arguing."

Max whistled and popped another chip in his mouth. "Damn. That was almost as sexy as Caius when he goes all growly."

Caius muttered something under his breath that Toua couldn't catch before asking, "Are we done here?"

Rían straightened and turned towards him. "I didn't need an entourage to begin with."

Caius raised an eyebrow. "The Order wants you dead."

"They what?" Toua demanded sharply, but Rían hissed and refused to meet his eyes. "Is that what happened to your leg?"

Rían deflated with a grimace. "They sent Reaper after me."

"And you *lived*?" The Reaper didn't fail. Any mage he targeted vanished without a trace.

"Of course I lived." Rían lifted his chin with an offended sneer, but Toua didn't buy it. As impressive as that was, winning had obviously come at a cost.

"Is there anything left you need to do here today?" Caius pressed.

"The logo," Max said and retrieved a small jar from the bags they'd brought in. "They didn't have grax, but here's the dogbane."

Toua stared at the jar filled clear to the top with tiny pink flower buds.

"Did you buy their whole fecking supply?" Rían asked, pitch rising with incredulity.

Max shrugged. "Yeah?"

Toua stifled a laugh and doctored the last hotdog while Rían muttered a drawn-out curse in Gaeilge. He sat back and munched his way through a bag of chips, watching as Rían walked Max through grinding up several of the flower buds before mixing them with crushed mage ivy and a few drops of yarrow oil. Then they went outside and faced the window. Rían's voice was too low to make out anything but the lilting cadence of his words.

"So how do you know Rían?" Lukas asked.

Toua tensed, turning towards the sofa to find three shifters focused on him. "He was brought to the Order a couple years after I was."

"And you weren't bound?"

He hesitated as he glanced out the window again. Spilling mage and Order secrets was rarely a good idea, but if Rían trusted them enough to be working with them, he supposed he could too. They certainly couldn't be worse than the drug cartel. "There are a few types of mages they can't bind. Spirit mages are one of them."

"Why didn't they try to kill you like Rían?" Quinn asked.

"They sold me to the cartel to work off my brother's debt." Toua tilted his head as he focused on Caius, since he seemed to be the alpha. "Why are you helping me?"

Quinn snorted and answered instead. "Apparently our new motto is rescuing stray mages."

There was a sharp shout outside, and Toua turned in time to see the spell attach to the window, the concoction they'd made trickling down like syrup. In its wake was a large triquetra enveloped in flames.

Max bounced twice on his toes, but Rían waited until the spell ran its course before nodding in approval. The limp was still there when they came back inside, but it had diminished considerably.

"I can finish setting up later," Rían said, his fingers lingering on the door. A moment later the minimal wards came to life with a faint hum against his senses. "Let's go." He nodded to the bags and boxes in the corner. "And don't forget your small fortune," he added dryly before leveling a pointed look at Toua.

He took that as a *Get your ass in the car* and grabbed the bags of snacks on his way out.

Toua only considered trying to protest once on the drive, but even the adrenaline of being surrounded by a pack of shifters couldn't diminish the exhaustion and gratitude threatening to drown him. How long had it been since he'd found another mage he could trust? Even most of those he'd passed while on the run were under the Order's thumb, and he'd never dared approach them.

When they pulled up to a small mansion, a strangled sound escaped his throat. "How big is your pack?"

"Just us," Quinn replied, already at the back of the SUV and gathering the boxes. "There's some spare rooms, but none of them are furnished yet, hence the musical beds."

Toua followed Rían inside. They left their shoes at the door before Rían led him up the stairs to a bedroom and retrieved a laptop bag off the bed.

"Bathroom's there. I'll find some clean clothes for you."

"Thank you. For all this," Toua said, waiting until Rían was gone to steady his breathing. He closed the bathroom door behind him, stripped his grimy clothes off and into the trash, and climbed into the shower. The hot water drew a moan out of him, and he tipped his head back and closed his eyes as it rained down on him.

Eventually he found the shampoo and scrubbed his hair clean, grimacing as the cloudy water swirled down the drain. He couldn't remember the last time he'd had a proper shower, and even after he washed himself three times, he swore he could still smell the filth.

Clothes were waiting for him on the end of the bed. Simple sweats and a T-shirt, aged and worn enough to be soft. He dressed and headed for the door but stopped when he heard a soft chirruping sound behind him.

He turned and spotted the cage with a small tent swaying from the ceiling bars. A moment later a furry white head poked out of the opening.

"Hello, gorgeous," Toua said, tilting his head as the small creature launched itself to the side of the cage and clambered down to the door that was open. He crouched and offered his hand, surprised when the soft critter climbed right into it. And then he gasped at the strange pull-push sensation in his chest.

"Oh no," he groaned as the impossibility of a familiar bond settled into place. Spirit healers rarely found familiars because the connections between a mage, spirit, and a familiar was a delicate enough balance that few were ever compatible. "Please don't tell me you belong to Rían."

CHAPTER 8

RÍAN HESITATED in the doorway of Lukas' room as the wolf picked dirty clothes off the floor. "I can sleep on the couch," he offered. Really, he had enough money he could just as easily get a hotel. Every big city had at least one or two with proper warding for mages. The longer he stayed here, the more it felt like he was being drawn into whatever clusterfuck was brewing. He didn't believe in coincidences, and he had no doubt that he and Toua ending up here was due to some cosmic balancing among shifters and mages.

But just because Denver's dead zone had become a vacuum sucking in all the available mages didn't mean he had to live in a fecking packhouse while the vacuum stabilized.

Lukas straightened and gave him a withering look that Rían ignored. "Don't be stupid," he said as he stripped the bedding and dumped it in the hall. He headed to the linen closet, returned with fresh sheets, made the bed with military efficiency, then stepped out. "All yours. Don't make a mess."

"Definitely gonna piss in your hamper."

"I'll tell Toua about the kinkajou."

Rían spun with a hiss, but Lukas was already gone, his snickers echoing behind him. "Fecking wolf," he muttered, dropping his bag to the bed before closing the door. Then he shut the door to the en suite, unsurprised they'd spent money to give everyone their own bathroom, and pressed his hand against it to call his Sidhe.

He found some of his spare clothes inside, including sensible boxers that didn't have smiley faces on them. A quick sniff test proved they were clean but musty enough from sitting to need washing again. He tossed them over his shoulder and found his large box of amulet pieces tucked into a corner. After a few moments of rummaging, he came away with some rings and one of his last silver triquetras. He added a few cheap copper rings and plain circular pieces for Max to get a taste of enchanting.

His wallet with his ID and credit card was intact and sitting on the edge of a shelf filled with his spare jars of Absinthe of Winter. Not that they'd be much use in the immediate future. As he glanced around at his hoard of supplies and components, he thought he could rebuild the basics of his bag within a few weeks, if he had the time to dedicate to it. He didn't know what kind of crisis Toua was bringing with him, but it was sure to be a headache.

He stepped out and sealed his Sidhe, dropped his clothes and wallet on the bed, and pulled his laptop out. While it booted, he took a few deep breaths to focus.

First things first. He needed to order a new bag. Or three. He wanted a spare in case this ever happened again, and Max needed to start learning to use components if he was ever going to do more than set things on fire.

His laptop booted with a critical battery level, and he tipped his head back with a groan before plugging it in. Then he realized he didn't have the Wi-Fi password and rolled off the bed to find Max. That was when he felt the distinct flare of magic signaling a new familiar bond.

He raced up the stairs to the bedroom where he'd left Toua, who was now crouched in front of the cage with the albino sugar glider in his palm. "Are you shitting me?"

Toua jerked his head up with wide, panicked eyes. "I can explain."

Rían was momentarily struck speechless. He remembered always being drawn to Toua when he was in the same room, and that pull had been there earlier too, but it'd dimmed, as if hidden beneath the grime and the toll of obvious despair of the last few years. Now, fresh from the shower, that all seemed to have been scrubbed away for the moment, and all he could think was, *Oh no, he's hot.*

He pushed those thoughts aside and raised an eyebrow. "What's to explain? You've been claimed by the asshole of the litter. Congratulations. He's your problem now."

"I—What?"

As rattled as he was to find all three of his sugar gliders were familiars, it was more disconcerting how he'd ended up back here after Max claimed the last one. And now Toua? An experienced spirit healer half a decade older than him, finding his familiar *now*? That was as unheard of as a mage Sparking at twenty-two.

"Better give him a name," Rían said and turned in search of Max. Instead he found all three wolves and mage sprawled on the couch, locked in a debate on what to order for dinner. He moved to a chair with a roll of his eyes. "Would it kill any of you to learn to cook?"

"Like you're one to talk," Lukas shot back.

"I was essentially a hostage to the Order for fourteen years. What's your excuse?"

"Bad parenting."

"Uh," Toua said as he reached the bottom of the stairs. "I could cook."

Rían snorted softly as all four of them looked at Toua with various levels of desperation. "There's no ingredients, and you're exhausted."

"We'll get groceries tomorrow if you make a list," Max said before pointing at the sugar glider in Toua's hand. "Is he yours now?"

Toua glanced at the albino, then at Rían, then at Max. "I think so."

Max started to say something else, but Caius clamped a hand over his mouth before he could. That didn't keep him from trying, and whatever he said came out an unintelligible muffle.

Rían had a sinking feeling he knew what Max was trying to say. From what he'd heard, Caius' reputation with the military was spotless enough that even the Order hadn't been able to turn up enough dirt for any kind of effective blackmail. But no one took out and then took over a mafia family out of the goodness of their heart. That required ruthlessness.

Caius needed power, and here he'd already gotten his hands on Max. And now Rían and Toua show up? Rían wasn't blind enough to think they wouldn't be asked to join the pack.

"Why don't you order food so we can talk about a partnership," Rían suggested.

Caius eyed him in silence for a moment before turning to Toua. "What would you like to eat?"

Toua sank into the chair across from Rían, absently stroking a thumb against his sugar glider's head. "I'm not picky."

"The Korean BBQ place is good," Lukas said, pulling out his phone. No one protested, and ten minutes later their order was placed.

Then Caius turned his attention to Rían. "I assume you have no interest in becoming pack."

"Not especially," he replied slowly, "but once the Order knows I'm still alive, they'll make sure to finish the job. And they're not too fond of any of you. If you're really taking power here, you need experienced mages who can train Max. And it's always nice to have a healer on hand," he added, glancing at Toua.

Toua stared back with a blank expression. "I'm sorry, what?"

Max pointed to the albino sugar glider, then at Rían and himself. "Those sugar gliders are family and our familiars. They deserve to stay together, so you're both becoming pack."

"That doesn't seem like the smartest way to choose pack members," Toua replied.

"Nothing about this pack is conventional," Quinn said with a snort. "And not like we don't have the space, or the money, to get you both set up in your own rooms. Or room, if you prefer," he added with a wink.

Rían narrowed his eyes at him and made a note to put poison ivy in Quinn's underwear.

"That's… very kind of you, but I couldn't possibly—"

"You don't need to make a decision now," Caius said, "but the offer stands."

Rían slumped in his chair and propped a foot on the edge of the coffee table. "It'll be easier to keep everyone warded if we're all under one roof for the time being." With all the warding left to do on the shop, plus the more advanced security he hadn't had the chance to put in place here last time, on top of the amulets and putting a new bag together, he would be running on coffee and spite for weeks, but at least his leg wasn't quite as painful. Most of the energy his body had been wasting on healing could be put to better use now too.

He rolled his head to the side to eye Caius. "What are you willing to pay me to train Max?"

Max gave an exaggerated gasp. "You're not going to train me because you like me?"

"You already tried to blow me up. I want hazard pay."

"That was an accident!" Max protested as Quinn laughed, resulting in a quick scuffle with a protesting Lukas caught in the middle.

"I want to build a greenhouse out back, and a shed that I can use as a workshop."

Caius raised an eyebrow, somehow completely ignoring the antics happening practically in his lap. "Is that all?"

"For now." Rían stood when the doorbell rang, more surprised than he should have been by the four bags of food. Shifter appetites weren't something he had a lot of experience with.

Once the food was divvied up, he glanced at Toua. "I'm ordering supplies tonight as soon as someone gives me the Wi-Fi password. Besides some more incense, what do you need?"

Toua's aura flickered with half a dozen emotions, relief and gratitude and guilt among them, before he let out a shuddery breath. "Basic Hmong shaman ritual tools would be appreciated."

"I remember you had a sword."

Toua winced. "Yes. All my tools were taken by the cartel and kept locked up unless I was using them."

"You can come show me what all you need. Max needs a bag to start sorting out his hoard," Rían added, still unable to believe they'd bought out most of the shop. Hopefully whatever few mages passed through wouldn't need the supplies.

"You can use whatever I bought," Max said. "There were some weird glowing mushrooms that looked cool, so I bought all of them."

Toua made a sharp wheezing sound as Rían buried his face in his palm. "How many?" he asked faintly.

"I don't know. Maybe two dozen?"

The wheezing sound nearly turned into hyperventilating.

"What? They weren't that expensive," Max defended. "The cashier gave me a discount on everything."

Rían gave him a dubious look. "Tell me you spent less than fifty grand, and I might believe you."

Max glared. "Mage components are worth the expense."

He couldn't exactly disagree, but at least when he spent that much he knew the quality of the items were worth the price. "Give me your receipt. I'll check later to make sure you weren't scammed."

When they'd finished eating, Rían took their familiars upstairs to give them their dinner, then motioned Toua to follow him to Lukas' bedroom. There wasn't a desk, so he propped himself against the headboard and grabbed his charged laptop. When Toua remained frozen in the doorway, he patted the bed next to him. "I won't bite, even if I want to," he said, smirking when Toua's aura flared with surprise and interest. "Now what all do you need besides a sword?"

IT TOOK nearly an hour to track down authentic shaman tools, but they finally got most everything that Toua needed aside from traditional clothing. The items that took the longest for Toua to pick out were his *tswb neeb*—finger bells—and a *txiab neeb*—a large bronze circle with nine circular discs and ribbons of red and white attached. The rest of the items he needed were a sword, colored ribbons, a gong, incense, spirit paper, and candles. Then Rían used his go-to site for supplies when he was in a pinch and found they had the same bag he'd ordered years ago in stock, so he ordered five of them. He left off replenishing his components until he went through Max's haul.

When he glanced at Toua to see if he was sure he didn't need anything else, he was out cold. He was surprised Toua had lasted that long. If the Order sold him directly to the cartel, Rían couldn't imagine the last several years had been kind to him. He'd need a decade to recover.

With a small flex of magic, he got Toua prone and tucked under the covers without waking him, then spent some time with his one indulgence: reading dark monster romance.

CHAPTER 9

IT WAS early when Rían woke, his body still running on Order time, which meant four or five hours of sleep was all he could manage before he was wide awake. He left Toua sleeping as he used the bathroom and took a quick shower. Then he remembered he hadn't washed the clothes he'd found. Too late to worry about that now. He was sick of wearing someone else's clothes. He could deal with a bit of a stale smell until more important things were taken care of. Like caffeine.

He headed to the kitchen and started the coffee maker, then waited impatiently for it to brew while he rummaged through the cabinets to see what needed stocking.

Nothing.

Some salt and pepper and cinnamon, and not even the good kind. Some cans of soup and an unopened box of instant rice. The fridge wasn't any better. Cheese, eggs, and beer with some strawberries and blueberries. There were three loaves of bread on the counter, and Rían stifled a groan, tempted to throw them all away to ensure he didn't have to eat another of Quinn's grilled cheese sandwiches.

The coffee finally gurgled to a stop, and he poured himself a mug, then settled in the chair by the coffee table as he typed out a list on his phone. Spices for one, and a spice rack. Staples like flours, sugars, and rice. More fruit. All the meats. They'd likely need a large freezer if they had any hope of not ordering takeout every night.

He paused as he realized he was including himself in the future plans of the pack. Probably because he'd gone and suggested he wanted to build a greenhouse in their backyard. It was a necessity for any freelance mage, and he'd planned to set one up the moment he found himself housing, but he couldn't even convince himself that the greenhouse was for Max when Rían eventually moved on. He'd made the mistake of thinking he had a chance to fight back if he did more than simply try to survive, and now he was stuck with the consequences.

He dropped his phone to the table and wrapped both hands around his mug as he slumped in the chair.

It wasn't the worst idea he'd ever had, getting involved with shifters. This was a nice property. The land around it was clean, or as clean as could be expected in a large city, which meant working magic here would be easy, and as much as he distrusted shifters, he at least knew Lukas well enough to know he was fiercely protective of those he saw as his. And if Toua stuck around….

He'd what, pine after a traumatized mage several years older than him?

He snorted into his coffee before draining it and getting up for a refill. The front door opened on his way back to his chair, and he glanced over to find Lukas returning from a run. "Exercise is bad for your health," he said, sinking into the chair and cradling his nectar of the gods.

Lukas rolled his eyes before filling his own cup. "Shouldn't you be snuggling your healer?"

Rían raised an eyebrow, noting the faint spark of jealousy in Lukas' aura. He wasn't blind to Lukas' attraction to him, but he'd never encouraged it. Though he might have been guilty of the occasional flirty banter. Even for a wolf Lukas was stunningly gorgeous, and they had the same dark sense of humor and got along well. But what little attraction Lukas had for him paled in comparison to what he'd always felt for Quinn.

He sipped his coffee in silence, waiting for Lukas to sit across from him and take a sip before asking, "You wanna fuck?" He'd hoped to finally catch Lukas by surprise enough for a reaction, like snorting coffee out his nose, but the wolf froze instead, with the almost unnatural stillness usually reserved for when he had a sniper rifle in his hands.

"You're joking, right?" Lukas finally asked.

"You tell me. If I'm going to be staying here, we should probably address it."

Lukas made a face and slumped in his chair. "If you'd asked me a few months ago, I might have said yes," he muttered, scrubbing a hand through his sweat-damp hair.

"And now?"

Lukas glared at him over the top of his mug. "Now I'm not the only one who would have to agree."

Rían shrugged. "Are you going to ask them to?"

Lukas sneered his annoyance and took a gulp of coffee. "Is this a genuine offer, or are you going to say no regardless?"

"I have nothing against a casual fuck, so long as it's to get me out of your system and you don't expect something more." No matter how well they got on, he drew the line at forming a relationship with a shifter. Even if a binding wouldn't hold on him, a claim might, and that was something he could live without.

"Such a romantic," Lukas replied dryly.

"That's the point," Rían snapped, turning his attention out the large glass doors leading to the backyard when Lukas raised an eyebrow at him. Casual sex was one thing, but it always seemed to lead to someone wanting a second or third fuck and then rooming together. The Order openly frowned upon their mages fornicating with other mages of the same gender, but they secretly encouraged it when there was a chance of a baby mage coming out of it.

He'd lost count of the times a woman came to him begging to stay over when a man couldn't take no for an answer. The number of times he'd been ambushed by those men was significantly less. After the fifth one suffered irreparable damage to his testicles, they got the hint that it wasn't a fluke.

"So was it a relationship that turned you off relationships, or the Order?"

Rían tilted his head enough to eye Lukas. "What makes you think it was the Order?"

Lukas shrugged. "There was that woman a few years ago who went public about all the shit they do to mages."

"Amelia."

"You know her?"

"You could say that." She'd bunked in Rían's room for the two months before she turned twenty-four, fretting over whether she should contact the media or anyone who could help. Her father was a senator, so they'd both thought she'd have ample protection. She'd kept in touch after she left, a text every few days, but shortly after the news hit, she vanished.

"Do you know what happened to her?"

Rían grimaced and stared out at the backyard again, at the faint dusting of snow covering the ground with more on the way. "I can only assume Reaper got her," he said softly. Maybe if he had tried harder to convince her to live her life, to try to leave the Order behind and focus on a career as a healer, she'd still be alive. He shook his head and scrubbed a hand through his hair. Regretting the past wasn't going to help with shite, and there was too much to do if they were going to survive.

"I need to take inventory of the supplies and set more wards."

Lukas snorted. "You need to rest and heal."

"Can't heal if I'm dead."

Lukas grunted but didn't argue, so Rían found the bags and boxes stacked in the corner and started to go through them. Sure enough, he found three jars of biolume shrooms, kept fresh enough that he could see they were top quality. As he picked his way through the spelled jars and containers, he found everything he needed to put his arsenal back together and then some. He even found a few pounds of death nettle, which surely got Max added to some kind of watch list if the store was under any reliable oversight. With this quality of ingredients, he doubted it was even under the Order's direct control; they tended to keep their best components stocked at the prison they called their academy.

Once all the containers were tucked away again, it was still early enough for sane people to be asleep. He had plenty to do, but until he was back to full strength, he could only do one set of wards a day. He wanted his shop done, but he could admit he wouldn't be officially opening for business for days if not weeks, and having the place he slept Order- and cartel- and Reaper-proof was the higher priority.

Since he was getting hungry for decent food, he quietly rummaged for a hoodie in Lukas' room, ignored how it hung nearly to his thighs, and called Niamh with a low whistle as he headed to the living room. A few moments later she sailed down the stairs and crawled into the hoodie's hand pouch. Then he opened a doorway and stepped through.

CHAPTER 10

LUKAS DESCENDED the stairs in a bit of a daze and climbed into the shower to wash the sweat off. The weird mood that had settled over him like a cloak wasn't so easy to get rid of.

He should have told Rían no. He was happy with his arrangement with Quinn and Max and wasn't looking to juggle another relationship. Except it wouldn't be a relationship according to Rían, and he wasn't sure that made it any better.

He shut off the water with a groan and climbed out to snag a towel and dry off on his way to the bed. Quinn was still asleep. Sometimes Lukas envied his ability to go back to sleep when he woke in the middle of the night. He didn't bother with clothes before crawling in close to Quinn's warmth and hooking an arm over him, splaying his palm against Quinn's chest.

Quinn stirred with a soft sigh, rocking into Lukas with a slurred, "S'wrong?"

Lukas buried his face in red hair and breathed in the warm cinnamon scent. If he didn't answer, Quinn would go back to sleep and he could deal with it never, but he found himself answering instead. "Rían asked if I wanted to fuck."

A long moment of silence followed, but the sharp flare of surprise in Quinn's scent meant he was fully awake now. "And?" he finally asked.

Lukas rubbed his nose against Quinn's neck. "I told him I might have said yes a few months ago, but it's not up to just me now."

Quinn rolled onto his back and caught the hand on his chest with his own, threading their fingers together. "So you do want to."

"I don't know. I never really expected it would go beyond flirting."

"And now that it can?"

Could it? Lukas wasn't sure about that. He sprawled over Quinn's chest and pinned his hand beside the pillow before pressing his face into Quinn's neck. "He says he's fine with a fuck to get him out of my system, but I don't think he'd trust me enough for either of us to enjoy it," he murmured, closing his eyes as Quinn's fingers slid into his hair.

"Is that what he said?"

Lukas snorted, his lips twitching into a smile as the possessive tightening of fingers sent delightful shivers down his spine. "Yeah, why?"

"You are worth more than a quick fuck," Quinn growled.

"Am I?" Even though he expected it, he was still left breathless when he suddenly found himself on his back, his wrists pinned on either side of his head, and Quinn glaring at him with wolf-bright eyes. Lukas flexed his wrists even though he had no desire to break free, his breath hitching when Quinn's fingers tightened enough to leave fleeting bruises. "Are you pissed that he offered or pissed I want to say yes?"

Quinn narrowed his eyes. "I'm pissed that you think so little of yourself you're willing to treat a one-night stand like a gift." He leaned down until their noses touched. "Do you want him that badly?"

Lukas swallowed hard, struggling to think clearly with Quinn's thigh pressed against his groin. "It's not like that." He lifted his head to steal a kiss, but Quinn pulled back.

"Enlighten me."

Lukas dropped his head to the pillow with a groan. "Fuck. I don't know." How was he supposed to explain something he didn't fully comprehend himself? He was saved from having to explain for the moment when Max stumbled down the stairs and into the bedroom.

"Quinnnn, are you awake? Oh good," he murmured, joining them on the bed with a yawn before blinking as he took in their positions. "Oooh, can I watch?"

Quinn snorted and rolled off Lukas. "We weren't fucking."

"Why not?" Max flopped on top of Lukas to take Quinn's place, his fingers quickly finding Lukas' nipples and teasing them.

"We were discussing Rían's offer to fuck Lukas."

Lukas scowled at Quinn, then hissed when Max twisted his nipple before slapping his hand away.

"Why would he do that?" Max asked.

"Oh, fuck you," Lukas snapped, shoving at Max, who merely blinked at him.

"No, I mean why now? You've known each other a while. Was he waiting until he was free of the Order?"

Lukas huffed and rolled to put his back to Max, but that only put him face-to-face with Quinn, so he closed his eyes. He suspected Rían's offer had more to do with Rían being interested in Toua and not wanting Lukas to interfere, but if he was against relationships as a whole, was he going to make the same offer to Toua? That seemed like a disaster waiting to happen and was the exact reason he dreaded expanding the pack.

Quinn pressed closer and tipped Lukas' chin up to finally kiss him. When Max snuggled in against his back and kissed across his shoulders, Lukas gave up any further thoughts of Rían and his offer. He already had a mage and a wolf to call his own, and he didn't want to be dragged into whatever drama was sure to come.

CHAPTER 11

RÍAN STEPPED into the café a few blocks from his shop and inhaled the scent of coffee. He ordered the biggest size they had, a cherry pastry for Niamh, two ham and cheese croissants for himself, and a bag of various pastries to take back to the house. Food in hand, he headed for his shop to eat in peace while he set up what little he could. He organized the smaller amulets he'd accumulated over the years in the display cabinet as he ate a croissant, but his peace didn't last long before the door opened.

Two men walked in with a shifter in tow. Even if Rían couldn't see their dark auras, the literal shock collar around the shifter's throat let him know these guys rivaled the Order on the scale of scum.

He popped the last of his croissant in his mouth and discreetly activated a few of his amulets to protect him in case bullets started flying. "Can I help you?" he asked, crossing his arms on the counter with his best bored nonchalance.

One of the men stepped forward, pushing his sunglasses on top of his head with a smile that might have worked on anyone who had no survival instincts. His eyes flicked over Rían's face, where his stitches were visible since he'd forgone trying to hide them under a new bandage after his shower. "We're looking for someone," he said, holding up a picture of Toua. It was at least a few years old, likely taken by the Order before the bastards handed him over.

Rían raised an eyebrow, then gave a pointed look around the empty shop. "I'm not officially open, and I just moved here. Maybe try the police."

The man narrowed his eyes and leaned an elbow on the counter, angling his body to show the gun on his hip beneath his wrinkled suit jacket. Rían resisted the urge to scoff in his face. "I know he was here. His scent leads right into your shop."

"Maybe he was squatting here. I just started setting up yesterday." He tilted his head, looking over the other man and the shifter. The latter looked worse than the villagers in Brazil—worn and malnourished, with fear and stress and despair tangled through his aura.

"Look, if you're not going to buy anything, I'm going to have to ask you to leave," Rían said, pressing his thumb to the thin silver ring on his little finger. He turned a *fuck off* smile on the man still crowding his space as he turned the ring. It shimmered as it activated, then vanished to reappear on the shifter's pinkie instead. It twisted into place and disappeared beneath a spell to keep it hidden.

Rían felt the shifter's sharp, surprised gaze boring into his face, but he ignored it, refusing to break eye contact with the thug in front of him.

"If you see him, tell him we're getting sick of chasing him."

"Oh, sure," he replied with a nod. "Bye now."

The man looked around the shop in a silent threat, and Rían narrowed his eyes. He didn't have the wards in place to protect against a Molotov cocktail, especially if a shifter managed to break through the window, and as much as he didn't want his shop destroyed, the house wards needed done first.

Once the men left, he waited ten minutes, then closed the blinds and packed up everything he'd set out. All the amulets and tattoo supplies and spell components went back into boxes and into his Sidhe. Then he moved the counter stool in there. The tattoo chairs were bolted to the ground, and the sofa was too big to bother with or he would have shoved those in there too.

Once everything he could save was inside, he snagged the food and his coffee as Niamh settled on his shoulder. He stepped inside his Sidhe and shut the door, and when he opened it again, he was in the upstairs bedroom of the packhouse.

Niamh chirped and sailed to the cage to snuggle in with her siblings while Rían headed downstairs.

Lukas, Caius, and Max were at the island counter. Quinn was at the stove scrambling eggs, and he turned with a confused frown. "I thought you left."

"I did." Rían dropped the pastry bag on the counter beside Max.

"Is that my hoodie?"

Rían ignored that. "I just had a visit from the cartel."

"Are they still alive?" Lukas asked.

"I'm sorry, my first instinct isn't *murder*," he replied with a roll of his eyes. He glanced around for Toua but didn't see him. "Is Toua still asleep?"

"He was when I peeked in," Max answered, pulling out a chocolate cake donut. "Drooling all over Lukas' pillow too."

"Oh good, I'll add it to the hamper."

"Going to castrate you in your sleep," Lukas muttered.

Rían was about to say that would be a feat since Lukas didn't know what a pair of balls looked like, but Caius spoke before he could. "I assume you have a plan?"

"Not really. I put a tracking ring on their pet shifter, though." That got their attention, so he added, "They had a shock collar on him. I doubt he was there by choice."

"A shock collar alone wouldn't be enough to control a shifter," Quinn said, scraping a heap of eggs onto each of four plates.

Rían refilled his coffee and sank into a chair at the dining table. "I was thinking I'd track them for the day. See where they're staying. Try to get the shifter alone tonight."

"Is that a good idea?" Quinn asked.

"Fastest way to get intel," he replied, pulling out his phone to access the tracking app. Magic and tech didn't always like to play nice, but that ring had a tiny GPS tracker on the inside that worked well enough. It was *Magierseele* tech, so he wasn't holding out hope of it working much longer. The way the FBI investigation was going, the entire company was likely to be broken up and sold off piecemeal by the end of the year.

He sucked down more coffee as he saw the tracker lighting up a few blocks from his shop. Likely waiting to follow him when he left. Did they not know he was a mage? Except if they'd been chasing Toua for so long, who barely had the magical energy to stay alive, much less open doorways, they hopefully had a skewed sense of the average mage's abilities. Healers didn't need to learn to use doorways as well as those who were sent on missions. The worst a healer had to deal with was detached limbs. For the rest of them, being able to open safe doorways was a matter of life and death.

Rían tucked his phone away and looked at Max. "Come help me with the wards when you're done," he said, taking his coffee to the back porch. He tipped his head back as a tiny mage portal opened over the backyard. A moment later a package sailed through and landed in the melting snow.

That needed fixed first. Incoming packages needed to be sent to a small quarantined corner of the property so the Order couldn't deliver a bomb to their doorstep. That wasn't exactly the Order's style, but if they got desperate enough to send someone other than Reaper, all bets were off.

He headed to the package and crouched beside it, spotting the bright blue of the logo for the company he'd bought the replacement bags from. He snatched it up with an eager sound, took it to the porch, and sat on the bench swing. For a moment after he opened it, he wasn't sure what he was looking at. Maybe it was the wrong package, because everything was coated in red like ketchup. Then the unmistakable smell of blood hit him and his stomach twisted. He tossed the box aside, but not before he finally recognized the familiar markings of sugar glider fur.

He landed on his knees and lost his breakfast over the edge of the patio. The dregs of his dinner were trying to come up when the door slid open. He managed a hoarse, "Don't come out here," before he dry heaved. There was a flurry of activity inside before someone held a wad of paper towels out to him. He spat a few times in a vain attempt to clear his mouth before scrubbing his face and glancing up at Caius.

"I think Reaper found me," Rían said, trying to get to his feet, but he was too shaky to stand yet. He collapsed with his back to the railing instead.

Caius stepped over him and crouched beside the package with a low curse. "What makes you think this was Reaper?"

Rían tipped his head back with a rough laugh. "He threatened to skin mine alive."

How had that bastard found him so fast? He'd been shielding his loca—Except he hadn't. Not since he gave that ring to Toua. And he'd never bothered putting down signature-blocking shields when he first came here since the Order already knew where Max lived. He'd focused what little time he had ensuring threats couldn't get past the wards easily, at least not without causing enough of a commotion to alert everyone inside.

"Fuck," he whispered, digging the heels of his palms into his eyes.

"Go inside," Caius said. "Quinn, I need some gloves."

"Yep," Quinn replied.

Caius glanced at Rían over his shoulder. "Are there any magical traps on this?"

Rían swallowed reflexively, grimacing at the burn in his throat, and studied Caius and the box from the corner of his eye. He dimmed Caius' aura with a magic dampener until it was barely brighter than the surrounding sunlight, then turned his attention to the package as best he could without looking at it directly. There was a tinge of darkness around it now that the standard protective spells for delivery were broken, and a flicker of magic at the bottom.

"There's something in it, but it's not a trap," he said as Quinn joined them and passed a pair of disposable gloves to Caius. Then he turned to Rían and held a hand out. He let Quinn pull him to his feet and inside, where Max was waiting with all three familiars tucked against his chest.

The relief at seeing them safe and whole almost outweighed the guilt that followed.

Niamh chirped and sailed to Rían, and he clutched her against his chest, where she burrowed into the hollow of his hand.

Quinn nudged Rían to the couch, where he sank into the corner and pulled his feet up. Aradia and the albino landed on his knees a moment later. Toua would need to name him soon.

Lukas pressed a glass of water into Rían's hand. He took a sip as he absently stroked his thumb along Niamh's soft, warm fur, focusing on the quick rhythm of her heartbeat.

"We need to strengthen the wards," Rían said after a long moment, before clearing his throat and sipping more water.

"That can wait," Quinn said, still hovering nearby as if he expected Rían to bolt. Which might have been insulting if he hadn't just emptied a gallon of coffee in the backyard. He'd seen worse on his missions, but he hadn't been prepared for that today.

"I'm going to kill him," Rían snarled as the shock and horror finally loosened their grip enough for anger to take root.

"Kill who?" Toua asked, stumbling into the room with a yawn. His dark hair was sleep tousled, and pillow creases lined his cheek.

For some reason Rían couldn't look away, though he blamed it on Toua's aura. It wasn't nearly as bright as Max or the others, and it wasn't anywhere near as strong as it should have been, thanks to the potion Toua had been taking, but it was the deep, soothing silver-green of a spirit healer.

Toua sank onto one of the chairs and tilted his head with a bleary, concerned stare. "Who're you killing?"

Rían swallowed and tried in vain to stop staring. "Reaper."

That wiped the lingering drowsiness away. Fear lit up Toua's aura like a Christmas tree catching fire. "He's here?"

Rían shook his head, but he couldn't form an answer.

"He sent a gift," Lukas muttered with a dark glower.

"More than one," Caius said as he stepped inside. His gloves were thankfully gone, but he held up what looked like a postcard as he shut the door behind him. "It says you have one week."

Rían sneered. "Fecking asswipe." If Reaper thought scare tactics would work on him, he was wrong. A week was enough time to prepare, especially if Toua could finish healing him. He could only hope the deadline meant Reaper had nearly died and was still recovering himself. His bag had been full of enough lethal components, including raw aconite, that surely even a shifter with mage bindings would have suffered sustaining damage.

"We can get the extra security added to the wards today," he said, giving up any hope of his shop being done anytime soon. Not like he could run a business with an assassin after him. Once the wards were done, he'd have to give Max a crash course in enchanting. No way in hell was he walking into another trap. If both Max and Toua could add their magic to his amulets, he'd at least have some protection if Reaper managed to get him near another nullifying barrier.

"You should probably rest for a minute," Lukas said.

Rían bared his teeth in a snarl. "I don't need coddling."

Lukas lifted his hands with a huff and headed to the kitchen for a beer. "Do you have a plan, then? Or is this going to be another 'I'll figure it out along the way,'" he mocked.

Rían narrowed his eyes. "I never heard you complaining about my plans."

"I do have some sense of self-preservation."

"Enough," Caius said firmly, moving to set the postcard on the kitchen counter. "What are the chances he'll come here?"

Rían shook his head. "I have no idea. He was waiting for me in a secure room. I'm sure he'll have some kind of trap ready. All I know is he's too fast not to have a mage bound to him."

"Great," Quinn muttered. "Any way to find him first?"

"Not without his blood." He would have said more, but Toua's stomach rumbled loudly enough to get all their attention.

"Sorry, ignore me."

"You need to eat," Rían said. Aradia and her brother scurried to their mages as Rían sat up, thankful for something else to focus on. Toua's aura might be on the mend, but he was still in desperate need of several solid meals.

"We've got eggs and toast," Quinn offered, and Toua whimpered. "Yes, please."

Rían started to get up, but Quinn was already heading to the stove.

"If you're still okay with cooking and give me a list, I'll run to the store in a bit," Lukas said.

Rían swallowed the irrational irritation as Toua settled at the kitchen island. "I don't mind. It's the least I can do."

Max tapped a socked foot against Rían's leg, then waggled his eyebrows when Rían looked at him.

"Oh, feck off," he muttered, getting to his feet. Niamh tucked herself into the hoodie pouch as he grabbed the jars of powdered ghost tongue and silent milfoil from beside the door.

Max laughed and followed him outside. "So what exactly are we doing?"

"Several things," Rían answered, moving to the back of the property line at the fence. "A ward to automatically shield the presence and signature of everyone who's here for starters. Another to prevent scrying or tracking in case the shielding is bypassed. And more of the protections like I put on the sitting room and house itself that keep your magic from running amok." He'd have to find his supply of condensed starlight for that one, as it wasn't something easily obtained, much less sold in stores, but the others were simple enough.

He held up the ghost tongue. "Aside from death nettle, this is one of the more dangerous components used on the regular. Even breathing it in can cause confusion, amnesia, or hallucinations."

Max stepped back. "And you're going to open it?"

Rían fought a faint smile and held it out. "No, you are."

"The fuck I am."

"Max," he said, the shock of Reaper's gift and the lingering ache in his leg and stinging in his cheek making it difficult to hold onto his patience. The cold was making it even worse. "The wards are already there. All you need to do is wrap your magic around a bit of the powder and feed it into them with the intention of obscuring those inside their boundary."

Max eyed him with distrust, and he fought the urge to roll his eyes.

"Like this," he said, cracking the lid open to create a sliver of space. He hovered his hand over it and reached for a pinch of powder. It wasn't until Max frowned in confusion that Rían realized he'd taken several steps for granted. Max had never been taught how to access the Spark of magic that fed his flames. Or how to call on the raw energy to use as a component in the more mundane spell castings. Both were usually some of the first things taught to new mages brought into the Order, but Max didn't even have a few years of experience of learning the limits of his magic on his own.

"Never mind," he said. "Let's start with the basics."

CHAPTER 12

TOUA TRIED to eat the massive plate of eggs and toast Quinn set in front of him; he really did. It'd been months since he'd had so much food available to him, but his stomach threatened to pop long before he finished. He hated to see food go to waste, but Quinn solved the problem by snatching the plate when Toua pushed it away and eating what was left. When Lukas grabbed his keys, Toua straightened and cleared his throat. "If I can borrow some clean clothes, I can help with the groceries."

Lukas glanced at Quinn, who shrugged and looked at Caius, who stood at the back door watching Max and Rían.

"All three of you go," Caius said over his shoulder. "I don't want anyone going out alone. Even for a run."

Lukas grumbled under his breath and turned pleading eyes on Quinn, who whined.

"Ask Max first. He likes getting up early." He dumped his plate in the sink and motioned Toua to follow him downstairs into a comfortable lair, complete with a multicomputer system in the corner to the right and a large sofa and entertainment center to the left.

Quinn disappeared into the bedroom on the other side of the gaming area and returned shortly with jeans and a hoodie. "We'll pick up some clothes for you while we're out, but I have a feeling a proper shopping trip will need to wait."

"Thank you." Toua wasn't quite sure how he'd ended up here, but the forces of the universe were never wrong. If he was meant to stop running, he was grateful for the reprieve. And that he'd reconnected with Rían. When he'd left the Order, Rían was a quiet and focused kid just starting solo missions. He wasn't at all surprised to find he'd become a serious and talented mage.

Toua changed as Quinn headed upstairs, then folded the clothes he'd slept in and took them up to the bedroom he should have slept in. When he rejoined Quinn and Lukas downstairs, the—*his* albino sugar glider climbed into the hoodie's pouch. A few minutes later he was in the back of an SUV. "Thank you again," he said quietly. "I doubt I'll be able to repay you for this."

They were likely only interested in his healing abilities, but they still could have easily abducted him instead of helping. Even putting him in a hotel room for a night would have been more than anyone else had done. Casually offering him a home was a bit too much to believe.

Quinn flicked his fingers in a dismissive gesture. "Don't worry about it. Cap apparently has a thing for taking in strays."

He wondered if Rían counted as a stray, but he hadn't seemed too eager to join the pack. Toua had never interacted much with shifters before the Order sold him out. The cartel had somehow kept two as hostages and were using them to help track him, but he'd never heard how that happened. Caleb had shown up about a year ago, a collar with a powerful spell already in place, and Dante showed up two days later. After an hour of negotiations, Dante had let them take the collar from Caleb and put it on him instead, and Caleb's had been replaced with a smaller shock collar.

Toua had caught sight of Caleb a few times over the past few months, and he was fairly certain the wolf was doing everything he could to keep the assholes chasing Toua from catching him. Toua couldn't blame him. He'd never heard either of them talk thanks to their collars, but it was obvious they cared for each other. If he were in Caleb's shoes, he'd want to keep them on the road as long as possible in the hopes of finding a way to escape.

They would hunt Toua down until they caught him or the cancer finally won. And if that happened, he was as good as dead. Any day now he expected to turn the corner and find the barrel of a gun waiting for him.

He instinctively watched the street names as they passed, noting the bus stops and what seemed like the quickest way to get to them. By the time they parked and climbed out, he had a decent idea of which direction they'd come from and how to get back to the neighborhood if he had to.

Quinn and Lukas each grabbed a cart and split up. Toua followed Quinn to the clothes section, where he grabbed a few cheap T-shirts, sweats, a pair of jeans, and a hoodie. He didn't bother checking anything but the sizes to make sure they were big enough. He found a pair of shoes that were comfortable since his were so worn down he could feel the texture of concrete through the soles. A pack each of socks and boxers, and he called it good.

When they found Lukas he was in the spice aisle, staring at his phone with an annoyed scowl. He picked up what looked like one of everything and tossed them into the cart to join the bags of chips, bread, and beer.

"Grab whatever you're comfortable making. Usually we subsist on grilled cheese, breakfast foods, and takeout," Quinn said.

Toua hesitated to choose too much, but the more junk or prepackaged food that went into the carts, the more he was convinced this was at least part of why he'd been led here. As a healer he knew the difference fresh ingredients could make, and if Reaper, the cartel, and the Order were coming for them, they'd need every advantage they could get.

Qhaub piaj was simple enough to make, both in quantity and that as a soup it was a forgiving recipe, so he tossed in several bags each of rice flour and tapioca starch for fresh noodles. Found the sweet soy sauce, oyster sauce, and chili garlic oil. A large container of bouillon powder, chicken broth, and a few giant bags of short grain white rice. He grabbed some other oils and sauces he liked to use while he was at it, and since Lukas already took care of the seasonings, he headed to the fresh ingredients, where he snagged some cilantro and green onion. When he saw the tofu, he couldn't resist grabbing some for the future.

"You have a large enough pot for soup, right?" he asked.

Quinn and Lukas glanced at each other. "Pretty sure we only bought some pans," Lukas said. "How big do you need?"

"A stock pot. Or however big you think it would take to feed everyone."

Lukas handed his cart to Toua and took off, so Toua returned to adding more fresh herbs and produce. Even if he didn't need them for qhaub piaj, he could use them in some other quick dishes later. His sugar glider jumped out of the pouch long enough to loudly demand some bok choy before climbing back inside, which Toua took as another sign that he was where he was meant to be.

Quinn added what little fruit was in season, and then they headed for the meat section, where he added several pounds of ground pork for meatballs before Quinn stopped him.

"Max doesn't eat pork."

"Oh. Is that the only thing I need to worry about?" he asked, trading them out for ground beef instead.

"The rest of us will eat just about anything. Not sure about Rían, though."

Toua nodded and picked out packages of boneless, skinless chicken thighs and breasts. Usually he'd use the bone-in, but he didn't want to deal with the extra work. Quinn added a few gallons of milk and way too much cheese for even six people.

He grabbed some parchment paper and foil when they passed the aisle in their search of Lukas and found him with another cart filled with two stock pots, a wok, and a rice cooker.

"Is this enough?"

"More than enough," Toua replied faintly, hoping that didn't mean he'd need to make two large stock pots worth of soup, but he had a feeling he was underestimating how much three healthy shifters could eat. Caleb and Dante had never seemed to eat much, but they were also stuck between being terrified for their lives and depressed, neither of which encouraged an appetite.

Checking out took forever, and the SUV barely held it all, but they managed.

His energy was waning by the time they got back to the house and put everything away, but he wanted his mother's thick chicken noodle soup so badly he started setting out what he needed to make it. He wasn't expecting any help, especially when both his sugar glider and Lukas disappeared the moment they could, but Quinn washed the pots, then propped a hip against the counter.

"I'll ruin the food if I try to cook it, but I can prep or measure ingredients if you need help."

"Yes, please," Toua said, nearly sagging with relief. He directed Quinn to fill a pot with all the broth and another with some water, then set them both to start heating. He dumped in the chicken, then made meatballs with the ground beef and some seasonings and put them in with the chicken while Quinn mixed equal parts rice flour and tapioca starch.

Toua added the boiling water and some oil to the mixture, stirred until it was a dough, then laid out some parchment paper. It wasn't until he had some of the dough set out that he realized if they hadn't had pots before now, they likely didn't have a cutting board or rolling pin either, which Quinn confirmed with a bemused shrug.

"None of us ever really learned to cook. Max would probably be interested in learning, though."

"Are they still working on the wards?"

Quinn tilted his head as if listening for something. "They're upstairs arguing about something magic adjacent."

Toua snorted softly and pulled out a beer bottle to use in place of a rolling pin. While he cut what felt like hundreds of long strips of thick noodles, Quinn told him stories of his time in the Marines with Caius and Lukas, and Toua found himself relaxing and laughing for the first time in years.

When the meat was cooked, he let Quinn shred the chicken while he took a break and drank some water. Max and Rían joined them, settling at the counter beside Toua.

"That smells good," Max said.

"It's about to smell even better." Toua added water to the pot as Quinn dumped the shredded chicken back in, tossed in a few heaping spoonfuls of bouillon powder, and brought it to a boil before the noodles went in. Then all that was left was to wait for the noodles to cook, though he was far more exhausted than he should have been. He'd been running on so little sleep for long enough that getting a full night's rest for once reminded his body of its limits.

He didn't realize he was listing to the side until Quinn slung an arm around his shoulders and guided him to the sofa, where he half collapsed into the corner. "Don't let the soup burn."

Quinn snorted. "I can at least do that much."

Toua hoped so, since he doubted he'd be getting up again for a while. The moment he sat, his body turned into limp noodles. Which was concerning since he'd wanted to finish healing Rían's leg and face, but he could do that tonight. He closed his eyes and let the soft murmur of conversation settle around him like a blanket.

SOMETHING POKED his cheek, and he startled awake to find striking crimson eyes hovering above him. "Wh's wrong?"

"Nothing. I got outvoted on letting you rest more," Rían replied dryly. "Soup's done, and it's late enough the wolves are getting hangry."

"Fuck off, squirrel."

Rían smirked and lifted his finger as if making his point. "See?"

Toua snickered. He knew he should get up, but Rían was still leaning over him, and the sunset coming through the back door was doing interesting things to the gold flecks in his eyes and highlighting the red undertones in his brown hair. Toua curled his fingers against his chest to fight the sudden urge to run them through it, which was a curious feeling. He found others aesthetically pleasing to look at, and every man in this pack was certainly worth a second or fifth look, but rarely did he feel any inclination to act on it.

Except when Rían's gaze flicked to Toua's lips before he quickly straightened, Toua found himself wondering what Rían tasted like. He lay there wondering long enough that Max leaned over the sofa with a sugar glider nestled in his hair.

"Are you coming?"

"Yeah." He rolled off the couch with a groan and checked to make sure the noodles were floating and translucent, but it'd been simmering for at least a few hours. He hadn't meant to fall asleep, much less for that long.

He sliced up some green onions, chopped some cilantro, and set out the chili garlic oil and sweet soy sauce, then turned to find everyone lingering at the island counter, watching him, as if waiting to be shown what to do. He grabbed a bowl, filled it with soup, and added a bit of everything on top. Then he took a small sip from the bowl before adding more chili oil.

Quinn started filling bowls and passing them out, and Toua stepped out of the way to settle on the far side of the dining table.

He propped his chin in his palm as he watched Max pour a drop of chili oil on his finger and lick it off, then do the same with the soy sauce. Rían added cilantro to his soup, but Toua noticed that no one else touched it. Then he gave up watching the others when Rían sat next to him, his entire focus shifting as if drawn by a magnet. It was incredibly hard not to stare.

Rían stirred his soup before taking a bite, then sat up straight and turned to Toua in surprise.

"What?" he asked, worried he'd messed up the recipe, but it tasted fine to him.

"This is a potion."

Toua glanced at their bowls of soup. "What?"

"How'd you make a potion out of soup?" Max asked, settling across from Toua.

"I didn't?"

Rían snorted softly. "You did. This is infused with layers of healing energy."

"So this'll heal your leg?" Quinn asked, sitting on Toua's other side.

"A little, yes."

Toua was too busy staring at his soup to pay much attention, but if that were true, that might explain why no one in the cartel had ever gotten sick while he'd been there, and their injuries healed far faster than he usually meant for them to. And maybe it explained why he always felt refreshed after eating food he'd made himself, even when he should have been exhausted.

Rían nudged his foot and tilted his head in question when Toua looked up.

He shook his head and ate, closing his eyes with a soft hum of bliss as the taste of home settled him. It might have only been because he was looking for the effects, but the warmth of the broth and spice of the oil spread through his chest and along his limbs and eased the deep discomfort where his magic Sparked inside him.

It was only then that he noticed the damage caused by suppressing his magic with that potion, and he hoped it wasn't permanent.

"This is almost more delicious than sushi," Quinn said before tipping his bowl back and draining the last of his broth. Then he got up for a refill, followed by Lukas. Caius and Max weren't far behind, but Toua didn't consider it a win until Rían filled a second bowl.

After they'd all eaten their fill, the soup that should have easily fed a dozen people was completely gone, and the thought of consistently preparing meals for a pack of shifters made him slump against the table with a groan. "You all eat too much."

Max snickered. "Yeah, I still can't believe they're not all fat and round like pandas."

"Excuse you, I'd make an adorable panda. A red panda," Quinn scoffed.

"Those aren't fat."

Caius closed his eyes briefly with the air of a man who was intimately familiar with futility.

Toua tuned out the rest of their banter when Rían's phone chimed, his attention shifting to Rían as he tapped the screen a few times, then let out a curious hum. "What is it?"

Rían glanced up with a smug smirk. "My tracker's been at a new location for an hour. Looks like a hotel."

IT DIDN'T take long to pinpoint the hotel and the room from the coordinates on the tracker. Rían waited another hour to ensure they were settled in and used the time to get more information from Toua, which wasn't much. Only that Caleb and Dante had shown up about a year ago and didn't talk due to the shock collars around their throats. Who they were or why they were there were questions he'd never gotten answers to.

When he was sure they were at the hotel for the night, Rían opened a tiny window portal large enough to poke his head through.

It looked like a typical hotel room, though it certainly wasn't the Ritz-Carlton. When he saw only two shifters inside on the bed, he waited long enough to make sure they wouldn't be interrupting anything before he pulled back and closed the window.

"Should be clear," he said, glancing at Lukas, who'd insisted he go as backup.

Toua crossed his arms. "I still think I should come. They may need healing. And they know me."

"You're the one the bastards are after," Rían said, striving for patience. Lukas raised an eyebrow at him, and Rían knew himself well enough to realize if it'd been anyone else being so stupid, he would have chewed them up one side and down the other. Lukas silently calling him out on it only served to annoy him further. "Let's go," he muttered, opening a proper doorway and stepping through.

The shifters were still on the bed. The one Rían had seen in his shop, Caleb, was sprawled facedown on top of the other, his body slack with deep sleep. The gray edges around his aura told Rían it was a drugged sleep, and he narrowed his eyes as he focused on the other one, who was awake and staring at them with sharp blue eyes, his limbs wrapped protectively around Caleb.

The matching shock collar around his throat wasn't surprising, but a moment later, Rían froze. He quickly reached out to stop Lukas from getting closer as he recognized the very illegal magical bomb woven into the collar.

That certainly changed things. He glanced around the room, enhancing his eyes briefly, enough to catch the glimmer of auras through the wall to the next room. They matched the cartel assholes who'd tried to threaten him, and they were currently reclining on their beds. He let the enhancement spell go as he turned back to the shifters. "You're Dante?"

The shifter narrowed his eyes, nostrils flaring as he took a deep breath. He scowled for a moment, likely catching Toua's scent, but he nodded.

"I assume if you speak, the collar goes off?" he asked quietly. Another nod. Rían spotted the paper pad and pen by the phone and handed them to Lukas, who at least knew him well enough to take them to Dante instead of asking questions. "Can you write down anything that might help us? Like where the keys for the collars are?"

That answer came first, a simple *Not here* in a handwriting as sharp as Dante's eyes. *He talks, he's shocked. They only let me see him when drugged. No keys. One has button that sets it off, uses it when they give him back to me.* Dante's letters turned darker and more jagged with the frustration and helpless anger that was lighting up as dark reds and oranges in his aura. *Leave me in a room when hunting the mage.* Dante snarled silently as he finished and looked up.

"How are they tracking Toua? When he changes cities or states."

Dante sighed. *Amulet but complained it wasn't working anymore.*

Well, at least his shielding was working. That might buy them a bit of time, though Max and his pack were infamous enough by now that it wouldn't be long before the cartel tracked them down. Either to try to gain information or their help. Or because they found out Toua was involved with them.

"They'll stay here?" he asked quietly. "Until they find Toua or he runs?"

Dante nodded and shrugged. *Were ordered not to return without him.*

Lukas raised an eyebrow at him. "We're not springing them?"

Rían grimaced as he studied the collars again. The shock collar he could deal with easily enough, but, "That collar will detonate if another mage tampers with it." He might be able to rig a containment spell around it, but he doubted it would give him the chance. The bomb spell would activate the moment any other magic came close to it. "I don't think I have anything that can get you free right now."

Even the Order rarely used such tactics, but they also never needed them when nearly every powerful mage was under their control. "Do you know the address of where the keys are kept?" It might be a long shot, but if he could get into the house, he might be able to track the magic. Hopefully before anyone activated it. "And whether the mage who made it is there?"

Dante scowled and scribbled out an address in California, followed by *Healer was only mage I ever smelled*.

Rían nodded and studied Caleb for a moment, but there wasn't much he could do for either of them right now. If it'd just been shock collars, he'd have no issue destroying them and disposing of the bastards in the next room. "We'll be in touch," he said, and Lukas took the pad and pen back and ripped off the pages that were written on.

He opened a doorway and motioned Lukas through. He made the mistake of glancing back and saw Dante slumped beneath Caleb, his aura dark with resigned defeat. Rían forced his feet to carry him through the portal and closed it behind him. As much as he hated leaving them behind without doing anything for them, it wouldn't help anyone if Dante got his head blown off.

He'd find a way to save them. He was free of the Order. Free to work his magic how and why and where he wanted. If he was going to make Denver his home, he wasn't going to let assholes like the cartel have their way here.

As he stood in the living room and looked from one concerned face to the next, he knew he'd need an official pack to make even half of his plans work. "I have an idea...."

CHAPTER 13

RÍAN'S IDEA was absolutely horrible, and after sleeping on it, he couldn't understand why any of them had agreed to it. Maybe they were feeling the pressure from shifters being held hostage in their territory or Reaper's threats hanging over their heads. Either way, as horrible as his plan was, it was simple enough.

He went through his new morning routine of portaling to the café near his shop for coffee and breakfast, then went into his shop with the blinds down and door locked. He called his Sidhe and stepped inside, leaving the door open as he grabbed his stool and dragged it to the back where he kept his more valuable components.

Instead of wasting his energy on setting wards, he worked on a new shielding ring to replace the one he'd given Toua. Unlike the simple silver bands he used for most of his own amulets, this one was a circle of delicate, intertwined triquetras. The base design meant its magical aptitude was significantly greater than a simple band, and he would be able to fit several enchantments on it.

He started with the physical protection spell. Luckily he had some powdered void root in a small jar, which he opened, dropped the ring into, and gave a little shake to ensure it was completely covered. The silver of the ring glowed as he set the spells, creating the unholy impression of a dark aura emanating from the pitch-black powder. When the spells were set, he used a pair of tweezers to retrieve the ring and shook off the residual powder before setting it aside.

Next he grabbed his container of condensed starlight for the magical protections. He didn't have much left; most of his supply had been used when he did the first sets of wards on the packhouse. But he had enough for a ring and to set the same level of protections on the house's boundary lines.

He twisted the cap off and circled his finger in the air as he collected a tiny amount with his magic. The liquid glowed a silver as bright as the void root was black, and as the droplet neared the ring, it began to vibrate enough to give off a high-pitched whine. It grew louder as he worked to stretch the not-quite-a-liquid out and around the entire ring, until he was gritting his teeth against the sound to keep them from vibrating too. Working with starlight was exponentially more difficult with a smaller target, but finally it snapped into place with a quiet pop and tiny explosion of stardust in the center of the ring.

He blew out a harsh breath of relief as the power and whine vanished and picked up the ring to examine it. Still intact, and still enough capacity for at least two more spells. He put the starlight away and pulled out the last bit of mountain nightshade he had left, but all of his ghost tongue had been used in his panicked attack against that first shifter in Brazil. With a sigh, he wrapped a purple nightshade flower in a bit of cloth and pocketed it with the ring to finish at the packhouse. Then he grabbed a small crystal to tuck in beside them.

Since he still had a few hours to kill, he picked out some of his simple bands and started making basic protection amulets for Max and the others. Most of his own amulets had been recharged to full capacity, and he'd asked Max to feed some of his own magic into them to ensure the nullifying trap wouldn't work again. At least not enough to leave him completely defenseless.

By the time Quinn stopped by to pick him up, he'd managed to make two rings and a new amulet to replace the necklace stolen from Max. After that and the ring, he was almost drained, thanks to his leg still not being completely healed, but it would have to do. One thing was for certain: He wouldn't be taking healers for granted again. Denver was large enough that his quick search found a couple healers who worked in the city, but the Order still had bindings on both of them.

He grabbed his stuff as Niamh settled on his shoulder and headed out to climb into the car. A quick check of his phone showed the tracker on the move, and a few minutes later he spotted the dark car tailing them. "Looks like it's working."

Quinn checked his mirrors and smirked. "Love a plan that could blow up in our faces," he said with a soft laugh.

Rían curled two fingers through the red strip of cloth around his wrist and rubbed his thumb against the worn fabric. That was the crux of the issue. Hopefully the bastards were desperate enough to find Toua and drag him back to their boss that they'd trade both Caleb and

Dante for him, but they had to know no one would willingly hand over a healer. No matter how this played out, it was sure to end bloody.

"Which part are you worrying about?" Quinn asked, raising an eyebrow as he glanced at Rían over the top of his sunglasses.

"All of it. Most of my plans have always been to walk in, blow something up, and leave."

Quinn snickered. "Not one for finesse or patience?"

"I have plenty of patience," Rían said dryly. "But when the Order gives you a mess to clean up every few days, you finish as quickly as you can so you can get some sleep." He paused and curled his fingers tight around the red cloth as he turned to Quinn. "Speaking of…. What do you think Caius would say to declaring this territory as off-limits to the Order?"

Quinn slanted a startled look at him. "Is that even something we could do?"

"There's an old bylaw that says they can't encroach or operate in areas where the local government or established powers declare the Order unwelcome." That was one of the reasons Japan and parts of Africa never had to deal with them, but the US and UK had submitted to the Order long before the expanding world made it harder for shifters to remain as little more than urban legends.

Quinn laughed. "Sounds like a plan, but how would we enforce it?"

"That's the beauty of it." Rían smirked as Quinn pulled into an expensive neighborhood and up a gated driveway. "Most of the old bylaws are spells." He ignored the weight of Quinn's gaze on him and climbed out. The mansion wasn't quite as big as Caius', and there was construction equipment strewn everywhere. Part of the house was covered in tarps, and the garage looked like it'd exploded.

He let out a low whistle as they headed for the door. "Max did all this?"

"Not all of it," Quinn said. "He might have lost control of the flames for a minute. We were a little busy with some asshole the Order sent, and the garage blew from a couple of propane tanks that caught fire."

"You're all lucky to be alive," Rían murmured. Every time he thought about the power feedback between the four of them from the claims and bindings, he wondered how any of them remained sane.

As they stepped inside, he caught sight of the car that had been tailing them idling at the end of the block. He doubted they'd make a move today, but now they could easily verify that Rían had ties to the Savino family, the main power in play in the city.

Signs of fire and smoke damage covered the walls and ceiling inside, though it looked mostly contained to the first floor. Quinn spoke with a few people who looked like they were trying too hard to present as respectable security guards, but maybe that was Rían's bias, since he could see the lines of violence in their auras.

When Quinn finished, Rían opened a doorway, and they stepped through into the living room of the packhouse. If anyone showed up looking for them at the Savino residence, Max would get a call and they'd return to meet their guests. For now all that was left was to prepare for a fight, even if they weren't sure where it would come from first.

He turned for the hallway but paused when he felt the wards activate in response to a delivery spell. Dread twisted in his gut, and Quinn spun around with a curse, eyes scanning for a threat before focusing on Rían.

"The fuck is wrong?"

Rían raised an eyebrow. "What?"

Quinn pointed an accusing finger at him. "Something just freaked you out."

He silently cursed shifter noses and moved to the back door with a mental note to make himself a scent-blocking amulet. "A package was delivered," he said, glancing out at the far corner of the backyard, where all packages would be contained until he could verify they were safe. Three large boxes were toppled against each other, and Rían didn't quite stifle a groan.

"Come on," Quinn said, opening the door.

Rían followed him out after a moment's hesitation, and he was immensely relieved when the packages turned out to be the supplies he'd ordered.

"A sword?" Quinn asked, pulling Toua's sword out with a look of awe.

Rían snatched it before the wolf could try to claim it for himself. "Get your own."

Quinn smirked and tipped his head back to eye Rían with amusement. "When exactly are you going to get your hands on Toua's other sword?" The eyebrow waggle that followed nearly earned him a punch in the face.

"Fates help me," he muttered. He was surrounded by sex addicts. Bad enough he had heard Max and Caius going at it last night before he'd managed to put up a sound barrier. He didn't need shifters getting involved in his own sex life. His ears burned as he grabbed the other packages and took them inside, ignoring Quinn's laughter. If his hands hadn't been full, he would have locked the bastard out.

Instead he headed upstairs to Toua's room and found him dozing on the bed. He stopped and was about to take the packages to Lukas' room for now, but Toua cracked his eyes open and lifted his head.

"Back already?" he asked, sitting up with a yawn.

"Didn't mean to wake you," Rían said, but Toua waved him off.

"I've gotten more sleep the past two days than the past month."

Rían shook his head, refraining from pointing out that the rest was needed, and handed over the sword and box of shaman supplies.

Toua took them and set the box aside, resting the sword across his lap before running his fingers along the sheath. "Thank you," he said, tipping his head back with a faint smile. "You're staying here, right? After this mess is over with, I mean."

Rían hesitated and set aside the box with his bags before sitting on the edge of the bed beside Toua. "I was considering it," he replied slowly. "Why? Do you want to go back to your family?"

"No. I don't know," Toua said with a soft laugh. He glanced away, staring through the door with a thoughtful expression. "I don't want to go to France. I haven't exactly spoken to my family much, and I doubt I would be welcome," he added with a wry twist of his lips.

Rían didn't need to ask what he meant; he could see the threads of shame flickering in Toua's aura and how they were tied to his sexual identity. He assumed that meant that Toua's family was more traditional and frowned upon anything other than a heterosexual relationship.

"My life has never exactly been my own. I'm not used to making these kinds of decisions."

Another reason not to pursue whatever feelings he might have for Toua. As much as he admired Toua and crushed on him years ago, neither of them had any experience managing their own lives outside of the Order's manipulation. And honestly, he couldn't be sure if he'd still be alive next week. It was either sheer luck or Fate's hand that had kept him alive until now, and both of those were finicky masters on the best of days.

Or maybe it wasn't either of those at all, but a promise made years ago. He didn't realize he was rubbing his red cloth bracelet until Toua pointed to it.

"I can't believe you've kept that for so long."

"Of course I did. You said it would protect me, and it did. It has. Numerous times."

"I could make you a better one."

"I like this one," Rían said, pressing his wrist to his stomach.

Toua snorted, but there was a flicker of… something in his aura, there and gone too quickly to catch anything but the deep blue of emotion. He cleared his throat and set the sword on the nightstand before motioning to Rían's leg and face. "I should be able to finish healing you, if you want."

Rían swallowed his reflexive protest. They all needed to be as prepared as possible, and Toua did look to be recovering well enough that working his magic wouldn't set him back, but there was always a chance his healing would be needed for a far more serious injury soon. That was the inevitable possibility with a pack this small with targets on all their backs, and he knew from experience that Toua would heal anyone who needed it, even if he burned himself out doing it.

But he wasn't much use to anyone when most of his energy was going to his injuries instead of replenishing his reserves. "All right," he murmured. "Do I need to take my pants off again?" He meant it as a joke, but a flush of pink spread across Toua's nose as he turned to rummage through his package.

"It would help, but I need a few minutes to set up." He set down a new stick of incense, then pulled out the four finger bells he'd ordered. They each had a thick red string tied to them, similar to the one around Rían's wrist. Toua picked them up one by one and shook them, tilting his head as he listened.

They all had a different tone and pitch, but Rían had no idea what that meant. He leaned back on his hands as he watched Toua pull out similar thick strings of cloth in white and black.

The bell with the highest pitch got one of each tied to it before Toua set it aside. The other three he added a white string to; then he picked the two with the lowest pitches and settled them on his thumb and index finger, the strings scattered across his palm and hanging to his elbow. Toua closed his eyes and moved his hand in a steady rhythm for several long moments.

The cadence and sound reminded Rían of winter. "Sounds like jingle bells."

Toua opened his eyes with a grin. "They're often called that." He gathered the strings in his free hand and tugged them tight. "I can work with these if you're ready."

Rían stood and eyed the door before nudging it closed enough that no one could walk by and see him half naked. Then he dropped his pants, revealing his simple black boxers, and sat down. Deep bruising still mottled his thigh, and the puncture wounds were little more than scabbed scar tissue, but the ache when he walked was from the torn muscles that hadn't fully healed yet.

Toua picked up the incense and held it out to Rían. "Can I bother you for a light?"

He snorted softly and called a small flame to his fingertip, using it to light the incense. He took the stick when Toua motioned him to take it and watched as Toua settled his freed hand over the bruising on his leg.

Toua pressed his fingers as far around the wounded area as he could, then closed his eyes and began shaking the bells in a slow, hypnotizing rhythm.

Unlike the discomfort of invisible hands twisting pieces of his flesh back into alignment that Rían had experienced a few days ago, this time Toua's healing was far gentler and more controlled. The invisible hands were there, but they nudged his muscles into their proper place and corrected the damage done to them. If he unfocused his eyes, he could almost see the echo of a pale silver-white energy coiled around his leg and Toua's hand. When he tilted his head away and watched the play of magic from the corner of his eye, he might have mistaken the pale wisps for a small dragon.

He bit his tongue to keep from asking. Toua was chanting softly under his breath, swaying a bit from side to side as he worked, and Rían knew better than to interrupt a healer when they were attuned to their magic. So he focused on the bells and the incense and watched the dragon from the corner of his eye, absently hoping it wasn't healing him only to try to eat him later. As it shifted and pulsed, the aches and pain and bruises melted away until all that was left was their memory.

The rhythm of the bells and chanting slowed, then stopped, and Toua listed to the side as the swell of magic faded.

Rían reached out to keep him from toppling off the bed. "All right?" he asked softly.

Toua blinked slowly, as if coming back to himself, before looking up with a wan smile. "I'm fine. How's the leg?"

"Good as new," Rían replied, though his attention was on the warmth of Toua's arm beneath his palm. He didn't realize how close they were until Toua blinked and Rían could count the individual lashes. He swallowed and let his hand slip off Toua's shoulder as he pulled back. "Done with this?" he asked, waving the gently smoking incense between them.

"Not yet." Toua took the incense with a soft jingle of bells and reached his other hand up to lightly press his fingertips to Rían's cheek. Another brief pulse of magic had the stitches falling away as the deep gash across his face healed, and since Toua's soup potion had cleared up the lingering burns, Rían was finally healed and pain free.

Rían plucked the incense from Toua's slack fingers when he sat back and pinched the end of the stick to put it out. "Thank you," he said, handing the stick back. A tremor shivered through him when Toua's fingers caressed his palm. When he glanced up, Toua's dark eyes locked on his.

"You should stay," he whispered. "With the pack, I mean."

"Is that what you plan to do?"

"I could… if I had a good reason to."

The offer of something more was a sharp twist of anxious anticipation in Rían's chest. His hand twitched into a loose grasp around Toua's fingers as he swayed closer. Toua's gaze flicked to Rían's lips as he leaned in as well.

The door swung open with a perfunctory knock, and Max poked his head in. "Hey, have you seen—Oh." He stopped in surprise as he saw Rían, his eyebrows inching towards his hairline as he took in their joined hands and Rían's pants pushed down to his knees. "*Oh*. Sorry." He quickly stepped back and slammed the door shut completely.

Rían closed his eyes with a groan, reluctantly letting go of Toua's hand when it slipped free of his grasp.

"Sorry," Toua said with a soft laugh, refusing to look at Rían as he focused on gathering up his supplies.

Rían muttered idle threats under his breath and stood to pull his pants up. "Thank you again for the healing."

"Of course. Anytime."

Since the moment was lost, Rían picked up his own package, then paused at the door. "Do you trust me?"

"With my life," Toua answered without hesitation.

Rían truly hoped they were never in that dire of a situation. "I need one of your hairs."

Toua's eyebrows shot up, but he plucked a dark hair from his head and handed it over with an amused twist of his lips. "You're not using it for a hex doll or something, are you?"

"Please," he scoffed. "There are easier ways to torment someone," he said with a smirk, wrapping his fingers tight around the hair before slipping out of the room. He spotted Max in the living room when he reached the bottom of the stairs and shot him an annoyed look before turning to head into Lukas' room. He dumped the box of bags on the bed and looked them over as he loosely wound Toua's hair around his finger, glad to find they were all identical to the one he'd lost.

When Max knocked on the open door a few moments later, he tossed one of the bags at him. "Get used to keeping that on you," he said, setting the other bags aside before sitting on the bed. "What do you want?"

Max wrinkled his nose and tucked the bag under his arm. "Caius wants to know if we should set up another bedroom."

"That's a bit premature, don't you think?"

Max shrugged. "He makes snap decisions and doesn't seem to ever regret them." He stepped into the room and flopped onto the bed next to Rían. "You're staying, right? As pack?"

Rían grunted softly and looked away before he could get sucked into the puppy dog eyes. "The Order may have decided to back off on getting their hands on you thanks to your pack, but they won't give up on me so easily." And Reaper sure as hell wasn't going to stop until one of them was dead. He only had a few days to recreate the bag he'd spent years putting together and make more amulets for the rest of them.

Max might not have great proficiency with potions, but he had surprisingly good control over the flow of his magic, all things considered. If Max could learn to imbue the amulets with the spells they needed, Rían could focus on the dozens of potions he needed to make.

He blinked as Max waved a hand in front of his face and flicked it away with a glare.

"Why is the Order so obsessed with you?"

"Because I made it a point to be indispensable." And because he'd broken into the forbidden archives and learned the old bylaw spells the Order tried so hard to keep secret. He'd never mentioned knowing about them to anyone until he'd told Quinn, but even using his Sidhe to access them couldn't bypass all the protective and alert spells. He'd only had half an hour to cast copy spells on every book he could, and while he was sure he'd left no trace, his missions had become far more frequent and dangerous shortly after.

Max raised an eyebrow. "Uh-huh." He rolled his eyes and sat up. "Fine, don't tell me, but it would be nice to have other mages in the pack." He smirked. "And you and Toua obviously have something going on. Which is good, 'cause I'll set you on fire if you hurt Lukas."

"I'm so scared."

"You should be. I know where you sleep."

Rían snorted and pulled out the triquetra amulet he'd finished. It wasn't quite as powerful as the one he'd initially given Max, but it should suffice for the moment. Max wasn't nearly as defenseless as he'd been a few months ago. "Here," he said, tossing it over when Max turned. "Try not to lose that one, yeah?"

He grabbed one of the bags and shook it out, breathing through the lingering anger as he gathered the few jars of potions he'd put together. Absinthe of Winter and a few healing potions weren't likely to be of much help, but he packed them anyway before grabbing some of the raw components. He'd split Max's haul in half and organized them in his own spare jars so the ghost tongue was easy to find.

He took out the mountain nightshade flower and tossed it into his new mortar to grind into a fine purple-and-yellow powder. He added a pinch of ghost tongue and mixed it before setting the ring in the center. A gentle shake ensured it was covered, and a quick spell added the signature shielding protection. Once the ring was removed and wiped down, he poured the remnants of powder into a spare jar and sealed it tight.

Then there was only one spell left to put in place.

He pulled out the crystal and carefully knotted Toua's hair around it before setting it on the dresser. The hard part was fusing them together, but his spatial manipulation magic made it a bit easier. As he blew out a slow breath, he nudged the hair to pull itself into a tight knot and for the crystal not to shatter. It vibrated on the dresser with a low thrumming whine, but between one blink and the next, the hair sucked itself into the center of the crystal without leaving a mark.

He snatched it up with a grin, linked the ring to Toua's magic signature and the hair, and turned to open a doorway. Denver had a few rivers, but he preferred to find one far, far away. When he stepped through, he was standing in front of Skógafoss, a giant waterfall in Iceland, and the largest one he'd ever seen. Being even this close to the Order's home base made his skin crawl, but it was a risk worth taking.

The rush of the waterfall was deafening as he stepped close enough to toss the crystal into the tumultuous plunge pool. He waited a few minutes to make sure the crystal sank and embedded into the riverbed, then turned to step back through the doorway.

That done, he hurried up the stairs, marveling at how easy it was to move now, and knocked on Toua's door. When it opened, he held his hand out with the new ring on his palm. "Trade me."

Toua stared at the ring long enough Rían expected him to refuse, but finally he pulled off the simple ring Rían had given him and handed it over. "You're sure?" he asked.

"Positive."

With a disbelieving shake of his head, Toua picked up the ring and turned it over between his fingers as he studied the design. "This is worth—"

"Nothing, since it's already attuned to you."

Toua slanted an exasperated look at him. "This is what you wanted my hair for?"

Rían shrugged. "I needed the hair to make sure any tracking spells that latch on report you as being in Iceland." He couldn't quite help his smirk when it sounded like Toua swore in a language he didn't know.

With a shake of his head, Toua slipped the ring onto his middle finger, only to pull it back off with a frown. He tried every other finger before finally sliding it onto his left ring finger. He twisted it back and forth a few times before clearing his throat. "Thank you."

"Anytime," Rían said faintly. He backed out of the room and refused to think that the ring only fitting that finger meant anything, even if he didn't believe in coincidences.

CHAPTER 14

TOUA COLLAPSED to the bed once he shut the door behind Rían and pulled a pillow over his face to muffle his groan. What the fuck was he *doing*? He didn't often question the forces at work in the universe, but what the fuck? Even when he'd been trapped with the cartel, he understood it was to correct the mistakes of his own blood, and when he couldn't take it anymore and the overwhelming need to get out and away wrapped around him so tightly he couldn't breathe, he understood that too.

One person could only endure so much when their environment didn't align with their nature. If he'd stayed there any longer, he would have been overcome with despair, and he was no use to anyone dead.

But this pull of attraction to Rían? It could only end in disaster. There might have been only five years between them, but the last time he'd seen Rían, he was barely nineteen and fighting acne, though it had only taken him a month to formulate a potion that actually worked on it.

Besides, Rían couldn't possibly want anything to do with someone who had zero interest in sex. Toua had no business being drawn to him. Except for the weight of the new ring on his finger. He rubbed his thumb over the intricate design before slowly turning it back and forth, marveling at the gentle hum of magic surrounding it. At least four separate protection spells, all of them top quality, and Rían asked for nothing in return? It couldn't mean anything, right? It was only repayment for the red string of protection he'd given Rían years ago.

More worrisome was the way his dragon spirit was entranced by Rían; he'd been far more willing to heal Rían than anyone they'd healed before.

He rolled over and shoved his face even deeper into his pillow with a hoarse, frustrated yell.

Maybe he should just suffocate himself now and save them both the trouble and embarrassment. Except he hadn't survived the Order and the cartel to give up now when he could finally take control of his own life. And if he was actually going to do that, he needed to make a decision.

He knew this pack hadn't given him safe harbor out of the goodness of their own hearts. Or not only because of that. Healers were sparse even in the Order, and good healers who weren't bound to them were far rarer. From what he'd gathered so far, this pack was atypically small. Even with Max's raw power, it couldn't make up for the lack of bodies. The shifter pack the cartel was allied with numbered in the dozens.

Toua was needed here. Could maybe even make a difference here. And he was almost fully convinced that if he decided to walk away, they would let him, but he'd already decided to stop running. He wasn't exactly a fighter, had never bothered to learn potions beyond the healing tonics and poultices for the less severe ailments. Outside of healing, unless there were malevolent spirits around or he needed to call someone's spirit back, there wasn't much for him to do. As much as he despised the Order's way of doing things, he preferred being part of something bigger.

This pack had already defied the Order once. Maybe they were open to doing more.

He rolled off his pillow and stared at the ceiling as nerves twisted his stomach. He had nothing to offer other than himself. What money he'd saved through his years with the Order had been taken by the cartel or spent to get his family to safety. The last few hundred bucks he'd had was used for his hasty escape.

Whatever he decided, he needed to do it soon, but it could at least wait until morning.

AFTER BREAKFAST, he found two of the smallest dishes he could find and filled one with a bit of water and the other with a spoonful of scrambled eggs. He took both to the coffee table and knelt beside it as he quietly offered them to his dragon spirit in thanks for his help healing Rían.

Then he followed after Caius, who'd disappeared into his office a few minutes ago.

"Something wrong?" Caius asked, looking up from his laptop and several stacks of folders scattered on the desk.

"Do you have a few minutes?"

Caius closed the laptop and motioned to the chair on the other side of the desk.

Toua shut the door and sat, fighting the overwhelming need to adjust his position. For some reason he felt like he'd been called into the head administrator's office. He pressed his palms against his thighs and cleared his throat. "I wanted to thank you again for helping me out, and if the offer to join your pack still stands, I'd like to know more about you."

Caius sat back and folded his hands over his stomach. "Me or the pack?"

"Both."

"Until recently I was a colonel in the Marines. Quinn and Lukas both served under me. Lukas' situation is a bit precarious at the moment.... Technically he's been placed on pack leave from his unit, but unofficially he's listed as MIA. As for Max, he's inherited the trust his father left to his sister and will soon own several businesses used for money laundering. Among other things," Caius said, pausing to press his fingers against his temple. "His father was head of the local mafia, and we've been sucked into the power vacuum left behind."

Toua had picked up pieces of that when Rían laid out his plan to bait the men who'd been tracking him. Maybe he should have been more wary, but compared to the missions given out by the Order and the violence of the cartel, this pack may as well have been upstanding and law-abiding citizens.

He could easily get a job at any hospital in the world, but he knew that wouldn't work for him. He'd be reduced to a shell of a person within a week, trying to heal everyone inside. No, he preferred the idea of a small group of people he was comfortable being loyal to. Who would accept him as one of their own. Even better if Rían stuck around, but there was enough to worry about right then without adding a disaster of an idea for a relationship on top.

"If you can promise not to drag innocent people into danger with your plans, I'd like to join your pack."

Caius smiled faintly and leaned forward, resting his clasped hands on top of his laptop. "I have no intentions of dragging anyone into danger, but there are plenty of people waiting for a chance to eliminate us. The Order is at the top of that list. You understand the risks if you join?"

"Yeah," Toua answered softly. There was a marked difference between facing something alone and facing it with others at his side. He might not know exactly what that difference was yet, but he'd been alone long enough to know he didn't enjoy it.

Caius tipped his head back like a man going to his execution. "Before you decide, Max requested a change to the plans if you decided to join us." When Toua tilted his head, Caius studied him with piercing storm-gray eyes, as if assessing his caliber. "The biggest flaw with this plan is that you're the only thing they are likely to trade for, and it sounds like they won't bring Dante to any meeting, so we have no excuse to know about him."

"You want to trade me for Caleb," he whispered.

Caius hesitated. "As much as I hate trading people, yes. It's the only option that's most guaranteed to keep everyone alive. I need more time for the rest of my pack to prepare for a rescue, but if they drive you back to California, that would be enough."

Toua dug his fingers into his thighs and forced his breathing to remain steady. He might have been able to trust them to fight to keep him, but could he trust them to come for him? More importantly, could he live with himself if something happened to Caleb or Dante that could have been prevented? "Rían surely didn't agree to this," he said, glancing up when Caius didn't respond. "You didn't tell him...."

"No, and unless he officially joins the pack we don't plan to."

Toua winced. "You're prepared to deal with a pissed-off mage?"

"I'm hoping he'll be more interested in helping retrieve you than killing us."

He couldn't quite stifle his incredulous laugh. "He's right. You're all insane." He scrubbed his hands over his face, but there wasn't anything to consider. This was the path he needed to take. He stood and held out his hand. "I'd be honored to join your pack."

Caius stood and stepped around the desk to clasp Toua's hand in a firm grip. "We'd be honored to have you," he said, briefly pressing his other hand against the side of Toua's neck.

Something shivered along the edges of his perception. Not quite magic, or at least not any he'd ever felt before. It was like his awareness of Caius expanded beyond what Toua could see, a sense of the wolf's presence and location settling at the back of his mind. A moment later, three more similar presences settled beside the first. One gave off the impression of bright heat, and he had no doubt that was Max.

It was more strange than unpleasant, and he rubbed the back of his head as if that could relieve the peculiar sensation. That was going to take some getting used to, though when Caius suggested he see Quinn to put together a list of supplies, it certainly made knowing where to find the redhead easier.

He hesitated at the door and glanced back over his shoulder. With the rest, meals, and lack of poison disrupting his magic the past few days, he could sense Caius' injury more clearly now. "When all this is taken care of, I could look at healing your shoulder. If you'd like."

Caius stilled, his shoulders heaving with a deep breath before he looked at Toua. "Do you think you can heal it?"

"Not quickly," he said. "It would likely take several sessions and a few minor surgeries, but yes."

Caius nodded. "That's the least of my concerns right now," he said, and Toua had the impression he was trying not to get his hopes up. "Once the cartel and Reaper are dealt with maybe."

Toua nodded and slipped out of the office.

AFTER TWO hours of Quinn taking him from one site to another to order everything from more clothes and shaman supplies to toiletries, kitchen tools, and groceries, Toua was ready to bash his head open against Quinn's fancy desk. The constant sound of shit blowing up from the game Lukas was playing on the giant entertainment center wasn't helping the beginning of a headache either. The only consolation was that he'd found a nice altar made from dark ash wood that would fit in the corner of the living room near the back doors. He even found some small offering dishes to go with it.

"Last one, promise," Quinn said, pulling up a furniture site and clicking on the bedroom section. "Bed and dresser, and whatever other furniture you think you'll need."

Toua bit his tongue against a protest. If not for Max's clothes and art supplies in the room he'd been using, he would have been fine taking it as his own despite the sugar glider cage. Even the sofa would be more acceptable compared to the price tag of furnishing a bedroom.

He almost managed not to wince as he clicked through the options. He didn't have much of an opinion on what his bed looked like considering it was used for sleeping, but he paused on a vintage wrought iron bed frame with the head and footboards broken into tiny pillars. It was certainly not something he'd choose for himself, but he couldn't ignore the instinct that he should choose it in a king size. He stifled a groan and went to add it to the cart, only to suddenly feel like it was the wrong choice.

With a frown, he clicked through other similar styles and finally found one in a deep cherry redwood rather than iron. That one he added to the cart, along with the matching dresser and two nightstands. He spent another ten minutes clicking through the mattresses, giving up any pretense of picking it out for himself and letting the spirits guide him. Whoever the bedroom was for, it wasn't him. He had no idea how to explain that without sounding insane, so he trusted things would work out in the end.

At least the sofa was comfortable.

When he'd finished, Quinn eyed the cart with a surprised whistle. "Expecting a guest in your bedroom?" he asked with an exaggerated waggle of his brows.

"Nope," he said, standing and escaping before that conversation could go anywhere.

When he made it upstairs to the living room, he found Max and Caius there, dressed in expensive suits. "Date night?" he asked with a smile.

Max tilted his head towards Toua as Caius straightened Max's tie. "I wish," he muttered as Rían joined them. "We're going to meet the bastards chasing you."

"Quinn. Lukas," Caius called. Once they were all gathered, Caius looked them over before focusing on Toua. "Coming or staying here?"

Rían made a sound of protest that Toua ignored. He knew better than to tip their hand, but there was no sense in waiting here when he knew he'd end up there anyway. Better to save them the trouble, since he doubted Rían would willingly open a doorway to retrieve him. "Coming," he said firmly. Rían's loud hiss was full of disapproval and misgivings, but Toua pretended he didn't hear.

The same instincts that had guided him on the bed were telling him he needed to go, and he'd stopped questioning those particular instincts years ago. Fighting them only served to make his life more difficult. Or led to people dying.

He noticed Niamh and Aradia both settled on their mages' shoulders and turned to the stairs. "Yaj," he called, holding his hand out when the albino sugar glider sailed down the stairs. Yaj landed and raced up Toua's arm to settle on top of his head.

Rían glared at them all, but he opened a doorway with a muttered "Let's get this over with."

CHAPTER 15

LUKAS FOLLOWED his pack through the magical doorway into Savino's living room. The stench of smoke and cleaning supplies burned his nose, but it wasn't nearly as disconcerting as knowing something was going on that he wasn't privy to.

Max smelled like nerves and guilt, and Caius' scent was the same as when they'd set out on missions—full of stubborn determination. Rían was a walking bottle of irritation and worry, the sharp ozone of his magic roiling beneath his skin.

Lukas' fingers itched for his rifle, but he settled for resting his hand on the M18 strapped to his thigh instead.

Max and Quinn led Toua off to a side room where he'd supposedly be able to watch and eavesdrop without being seen. When Max returned alone, Lukas raised an eyebrow and glanced from him to Caius. "So what's the plan?" he asked.

Caius turned towards him, his gaze moving briefly to Rían, and Lukas didn't miss the subtle flick of Caius' fingers. One of the signals they'd developed for use during combat.

Whatever was about to happen, Rían was sure to protest, and Lukas was responsible for keeping him from interfering. Wonderful.

"Trust Max," was all Caius said.

Max ran his fingers through his hair and tugged at his suit jacket. He looked every inch the part of a mafia boss' son, and when he closed his eyes and took a few deep breaths, the transformation was complete. Max glanced over them with a distant, calculating expression he could have only learned from his father, lifted his chin, and turned towards the dining room, where their guests were waiting.

Caius followed close behind, and Lukas fell in behind them. Rían brought up the rear until he reached the entrance, where he stepped to the side to wait. Caius sat at the head of the table, and Max propped himself against the back of it like an interested sidepiece rather than the current head of the Savino family.

Lukas took his spot a few paces back, glancing at the four hired bodyguards spread around the room before focusing on the two men at the table. Tweedledee and Tweedledum, Toua had called them. The names seemed fitting. On their other side was a shifter. Caleb, the one who'd been in a drugged sleep. He'd smelled off before, but it was worse now, a nauseating mix of despair, sickness, and the lingering bitter scent of drugs. He was pale where he was all but slumped on top of the table, his breaths uneven and his eyes unfocused.

Caius sat back in his chair and crossed his legs. "What do you want?"

The man seated closest to them took in the three of them before turning a dubious look on Caius. "You're Savino?" he asked, and Lukas mentally dubbed him Tweedledum.

"No, but I'm the one you're dealing with."

Tweedledum narrowed his eyes but didn't protest. Instead he pulled a photo from his jacket pocket and slid it across the table. "We're looking for this man. He owes a large debt to our employer."

"Who's your employer?"

"Hugo Andrade."

Current head of the cartel based in Fresno. Toua hadn't been lying, though chasing him across the country with two collared shifters seemed a bit extreme, even if he was a healer.

Caius studied the photo without touching it. "And what makes you think we've seen him?"

"Your mage. He came here from a tattoo shop. He smelled like this man," Tweedledum said, tapping the photo before returning it to his pocket.

"Even if we've seen him, that information would have a price."

He shrugged. "We can pay your fee."

"I'm not interested in money," Caius said with a faint sneer. "As a shifter, the fact you've collared one of us and brought him here when he looks like he's courting Death is enough to make me want to rip your throats out." He leaned forward with a deep, threatening growl, his face partially shifting to reveal sharp wolf teeth.

Both men scrambled to their feet and reached for their weapons, but Lukas drew and aimed at Tweedledum before he could get a finger on his own gun. The sharp spike of fear sweat drew a soft growl from him, and both men lifted their hands.

"Now, now," Max drawled, straightening and pushing off Caius' chair. "I'm sure you didn't mean to offend us. I've only recently taken my father's place. How could you have possibly known I have shifters here?" He propped himself against the edge of the table in front of Caius and pulled himself up in a smooth motion. "Sit," he ordered, leaning back on his palms and crossing a leg over his knee.

The men eyed him warily but complied, sinking into their chairs and lowering their hands to the table.

Lukas waited a few beats before lowering his gun, keeping it pointed at the floor instead of holstering it.

Max's cold smile was unnerving. "You're interested in finding someone. I'm interested in this shifter you obviously have no regard for."

"You can't be serious. You want to trade a shifter for a— human?" Tweedledee paused briefly enough before "human" that Lukas suspected he'd almost said "healer."

"Seems like a fair trade. A life for a life. Or one life for three," Max amended, leaning a bit closer to stage whisper, "He *really* wants to tear your throats out. I haven't let him kill recently. He's getting a bit antsy."

"Let him?" Tweedledum demanded, as if that were the most ludicrous thing he'd ever heard. "He's not collared."

Max scoffed. "He's a bodyguard with benefits. Why would I need a collar?"

The thick scent of Caius' exasperation nearly made Lukas laugh, especially when the men appeared equally disgusted and intrigued.

"They're all shifters?" Tweedledee asked, glancing around the room. "You expect us to believe a human controls them without a collar?"

"Please, I'm not a mere human," Max said, rolling his eyes. "I'm a fucking mage." He lifted his finger and a flame sparked to life around it, which he blew out like a candle with a theatrical flourish. "And I know how to break bindings. You need proof?" he asked, and Lukas tensed when Max turned that smile on him. "Come here."

Lukas stifled a sigh and stepped closer, holstering his gun as he stopped in front of Max.

"Kneel."

He was keenly aware of numerous sets of eyes on him as he narrowed his own at Max. The sudden heat of a collar of flames was as surprising as the effect it had on him. They didn't burn, but he got the hint and sank to his knees, catching the brief, gleeful scent of mischief as Max wiggled his boot in front of Lukas' face.

"Now lick."

Trust Max, my ass, he thought, but he could put on a show when needed. Without breaking eye contact, he grasped Max's heel and lifted it, his tongue flicking out to lick the top of his boot, then dragging all the way up his ankle. He caught the faint scent of soap and tasted little more than treated leather, and he was going to kick someone's ass later for not letting him in on this plan. He sat back on his heels and released Max's foot.

Max smiled. "Good boy," he said with a pat to Lukas' head. The faint heat of the flames vanished a second later as Max turned to the men with a smirk. "Convinced?"

Caleb chose that moment to regain his senses. At least enough that he pushed off the table and rose partially out of his seat, his eyes focused on a spot beside the large wine rack across the room.

The men straightened as their dumbfounded expressions turned suspicious. "He's here?"

Caleb glanced at Max and Caius before dropping his gaze and nodding, the stench of desperation and guilt coming off him in waves.

Max sighed as if bored, bright blue flames erupting around his fingers before the men could do something stupid like reach for their weapons again. "Yes, we have the healer. And we've named our price."

"No," Rían snarled, stepping into the room as he finally clued in.

Max ignored him as he studied the men. "Take it or leave it. You have about thirty seconds to decide."

Less than that, if Rían's furious expression was any indication. When he reached into his bag, Lukas surged to his feet, grabbing Rían with one arm around his throat and pressing his gun to the mage's temple. "Belize," he hissed quietly. That was the mission he'd saved Rían's ass from a giant puma, but he wasn't sure it would be enough to make Rían trust them now.

Rían snarled, but he didn't throw the jar of silver-blue liquid in his hand. "Fucking traitors," he spat.

One of the men stood and pushed Caleb closer to Max. "Where is Toua?"

"Quinn!" Max called.

A long moment of silence followed before a hidden door slid open and Toua stepped out, his wrists bound with what looked like some of Quinn's Shibari rope. Quinn stood behind him with a gun to his back.

Max waved his hand, the blue flames whooshing through the air, before he pointed to the collar on Caleb's throat. "I have no need for that."

Tweedledum shrugged. "We don't have the key. You're a mage. Burn it off."

Max narrowed his eyes and slid off the table with a look he certainly learned from Rían. One that said he'd turn them both into bugs if it were possible. When he reached for the collar, the electronics sparked and fizzled, the plastic melting all the way through before it clattered to the floor. The flames vanished, and Max pushed Caleb towards Caius as Quinn nudged Toua closer.

"Don't," Rían snarled, managing half a step forward as he fought Lukas' hold.

Max ignored him and pulled out a small vial of blue liquid. Lukas was certain it was one of the healing potions they'd made before Max blew up the kitchen, but Max said, "This should put him to sleep long enough to get on the road." He opened it and held it out to Toua.

"Drink," Quinn snapped, making a show of digging the gun into Toua's ribs.

Toua grimaced and took the vial, nearly fumbling it with his bound hands before draining it. Then he threw it on the floor with enough force it shattered. "I hope this was worth it," he spat, swaying and stumbling forward a step.

Quinn caught him and turned him enough to put him over a shoulder, and Toua did well playing as unconscious deadweight.

Lukas felt the subtle twist of magic when Rían's hand flexed, and he barely caught the shimmer of something on Toua's little finger before it disappeared completely.

The men eyed them all one last time before stepping away from the table. "Pleasure doing business with you," Tweedledee said as Quinn followed them out.

Once the door closed behind them, Rían snarled, "Explain."

Max scrubbed both hands over his face, the cold mask vanishing. "It was the only way. You said yourself you can't get Dante's bomb off. We have less than twenty-four hours if they drive straight home to figure out how to retrieve Toua and save Dante."

Lukas carefully released Rían and shoved his gun back into its holster. "You could have let me know the plan."

"What plan?" Max replied dryly before pointing to Caleb, who'd collapsed into Caius' seat. "Do you have any more of those healing potions?"

Rían muttered familiar curses under his breath before digging out a couple of vials and pressing them into Caleb's slack fingers. "Drink these."

The thick stench of fear wasn't surprising, but it still made a growl build in the back of Lukas' throat. He crouched in front of the chair and waited for Caleb to look at him. "It's a healing potion, nothing more. We won't put you to sleep."

Caleb looked from him to Caius and let out a shaky breath before lifting the vials and drinking.

"The collar is gone," Caius said. "Was that the only one?"

The empty vials fell to the floor as Caleb pressed his hands to his neck and doubled over with a hoarse sob that sounded like it was tearing his throat.

Rían cursed softly and stalked out of the room. Max followed, and Lukas hoped they didn't try to kill each other.

Lukas gripped the back of Caleb's neck and leaned close despite the particular smell of someone who hadn't been allowed to shower in days.

Caleb sniffed and latched on to Lukas' arm. "You're going to save them, right?" he croaked.

"That's the plan. Can you help?"

He nodded and lifted the collar of his shirt to clean his face. "What do you need?"

"Let's get everyone back home first," Caius said. "You look like you could use a decent meal."

Caleb took a breath as if to argue, but he didn't. He didn't loosen his grip on Lukas either, so Lukas straightened and sat on the table as Caius went to gather the others, who were having a shouting match on the front porch.

"Why?" Caleb asked softly.

"They wouldn't have traded you for anything else." As much as he hated not being in on the plan, he'd known there wasn't another viable option. They had no way to free Dante if magic wouldn't work, and this way the bastards' guard would be down. They wouldn't be able to fly back to California, not with a bomb on Dante's throat, and if they risked removing it, Dante would certainly kill them with Caleb out of danger. Their only choice was to make the twenty-hour drive unless they had a mage on hand.

Hopefully that would be enough time to come up with an actual plan.

CHAPTER 16

RÍAN SEETHED as he paced the boundary of the packhouse living room, checking his phone every few minutes to make sure the tracker on Toua's ring was still working. If he hadn't been there to move the ring from Caleb to Toua they'd be in the dark now, and their blasé attitude about their lack of communication or ability to come up with a decent plan pissed him off.

Lukas was at the dining table with Caleb, trying to get him to eat the steaks they'd picked up. Max and Caius had disappeared to Caius' office to make some calls, whatever the feck that meant. Quinn was sprawled on the sofa watching Rían, as if expecting him to open a portal large enough for a car to drive through, which he was sorely tempted to do.

"You had no right," he snarled.

Quinn raised an eyebrow. "We already told you he agreed to it. He's pack, which means he's our responsibility, and we're going to get him back." He dropped his head against the back of the sofa with a groan. "Will you sit the fuck down? You're making me nervous."

"Good," Rían snapped and continued pacing. At least until Caius and Max returned, then he spun to face them with another snarl. "You better have a good plan."

Caius focused on him with a calm expression that was somehow chastising, but Rían was too upset to heed the warning. "That's what we're working on. We need you to open a doorway to these coordinates," he said, holding up his phone to show a map zoomed in to a spot in Wyoming's national forest.

"Are you going to let me in on this plan?"

"Yes, now please open the door," Caius said tightly. "We have little time to waste."

Rían bit back his curses and turned to the empty space in the living room. Once the door was shimmering in place, he expected Caius and Max to go through, but instead someone came in. A tall shifter, his brown hair sticking up in every direction and what looked like spilled orange juice on his shirt. Which wasn't nearly as surprising as the man who followed.

"Akito?" he asked, his worry and anger momentarily fading beneath the shock.

Akito pushed his sunglasses to the top of his head, making a mess of his black hair. "Hey, Red," he said, turning to Rían with a smirk.

"What the feck is going on? This is where you disappeared to?"

Akito shrugged and stepped away from the portal with a sharp whistle. A moment later his large cat familiar leaped through.

Max startled, pointing at the feline with wide eyes and an accusatory, "What the fuck?"

Akito's smirk widened as he patted the cat's head. "This is Rui. She's a Tsushima leopard."

"Cat," Rían corrected.

Akito flipped him off and continued. "The Order deemed her too dangerous to let her work with me and always kept her confined to HQ."

"Because she's a menace," Rían muttered, glaring at the overgrown cat when she turned to him with a soft yowl. "Is anyone else coming?" he asked. When Akito waved a hand, he let the doorway close.

Caius cleared his throat. "This is Leon. He runs my old pack in my place."

Rían crossed his arms. "No offense, but you look exhausted." That didn't exactly bode well for any plans they made.

Leon smiled faintly. "I have a four-year-old. Who was very angry about his juice this morning."

"Gods, that kid's lungs could set a world record," Akito muttered. He frowned at Rui when she prowled to the dining room, grabbed the sleeve of Caleb's borrowed sweater between her teeth, and pulled until the wolf stood and followed her to the sofa, where he sat with wide eyes. Rui hopped onto the cushion next to him and sprawled across his lap. She crossed her paws and rested her chin on them, closing her eyes with a deep rumbling purr.

Akito crossed his arms with narrowed eyes and muttered something in Japanese under his breath before turning to Caius. "So what do you need? You mentioned a bomb."

It didn't take long to catch them up on the situation, but Akito's scowl only deepened the more he heard. "You don't know who set the spell?" he asked.

Rían shook his head. "I didn't recognize the signature."

"Why not use that nifty sleep gas you like so much?"

"If I had three days to put it together, I could."

"What about the nullifying thing you mentioned?" Max asked.

Akito flicked his fingers. "Not enough time."

"And I don't have everything needed for one anyway," Rían muttered, checking his phone again. It looked like Toua was at the hotel, and Rían could only hope they waited until morning to leave town. Especially since it looked like their only options so far seemed to be either infiltrate the cartel's compound and hope they found the remote before it was used, or take them out with force.

CHAPTER 17

TOUA SLUMPED across the back seat and kept his eyes closed and body limp. He wasn't sure how long they'd buy that he was really unconscious, but he'd pretend as long as he could. Not like there was much else he could do. If he considered his situation too closely, the terror would take hold. The only thing keeping him relatively calm was the fact they couldn't do much harm to him. They needed him alive to heal their boss, but he had no doubt they'd put one of their fucking bombs or something worse on him as soon as they got him back.

Except that wouldn't happen because his pack was going to come for him. Even if he'd joined less than a day ago, they were pack. And Rían's furious expression when they'd handed Toua over gave him hope that Rían wouldn't abandon him either, despite the deception.

He absently rubbed his thumb against his little finger where he could sense the new ring Rían had put there and hoped it was a tracker. It was too much to hope for it to have a communication spell. Whatever it was, he couldn't see it and he couldn't feel it except for the strange weight on his finger.

The car stopped, and his stomach twisted with nerves when it didn't start moving again. When the passenger door opened, he risked cracking his eye open. There wasn't much to see other than a parking lot, though the hotel across the street suggested they were picking up Dante so they could start the long drive across the country. Apparently it was also too much to hope they'd stay the night and head out in the morning.

He was looking forward to Dante finding out Toua had been traded for Caleb even less than returning to California.

When the driver swore long minutes later and got out of the car, Toua carefully peeked over the seats. He only saw Tweedledee and Tweedledum yelling at Dante beside them. Dante, who was staring at Toua or something near him.

A knock on the window startled him into looking up to find the Mage Reaper grinning at him, sharp wolf teeth bared in a predatory grin. Toua scrambled back, shoving himself to the other side of the back seat.

The door opened behind him, and Tweedledee dragged him out. Reaper stalked around the trunk of the car, the sun glinting off the left side of his face where the flesh was scarred white. His left eye was missing, replaced by an orb that glowed an eerie black.

"Back off." Tweedledum drew his gun, but Reaper's focus was on Toua.

"Did Rían get my gift?"

Toua kept his mouth shut. Even if he'd known what Reaper was talking about, he knew better than to play the bastard's game.

"I said back off," Tweedledum snarled again.

Reaper turned his deranged expression to the humans, and even Toua felt their spike of panic. The gun went off, and Toua flinched as he stumbled into the car, his ears ringing. He caught only a blur of movement before he heard a sickening crack. Tweedledum fell to the pavement, unmoving.

Tweedledee had his own gun out and pointed at Reaper's chest. "Who the fuck are you?"

Reaper kicked the dropped gun away before considering Tweedledee. "The mage I'm after visited your pet."

Tweedledee frowned in confusion before glancing at Dante, who was still watching Toua, his eyes narrowed and teeth bared in a snarl.

"He's fine," Toua mouthed, but that didn't seem to be enough to convince Dante.

Tweedledee lowered his gun. "The mage with red eyes?"

"Oh, you've seen him too." Reaper crouched and picked up the gun, removing the magazine and the bullet in the chamber before tossing it through the open door into the back seat. Then he pointed towards Dante. "I smell another pet. What happened to him?"

"What's it to you?"

Reaper stepped into Tweedledee's personal space in a too quick blur of movement despite the gun. "Because I want to know why you're suddenly in possession of the healer I was told I couldn't have."

Panic flared in Toua's gut at the thought of the Order handing him over to Reaper. If he'd ever doubted the universe for ending up as hostage to the cartel, he knew without doubt it was better than Reaper getting his hands on him. Toua twisted his wrists until he could slip free of the rope. Quinn hadn't tied his hands tight or well enough to keep him restrained, though that wasn't much help now. He should have run the moment they stopped the car. Or when Max burned Caleb's collar.

They should have taken the Tweedles hostage instead. Made them call their boss to free Dante, then sent them back empty-handed. Except Hugo was more likely to activate the bomb than free someone without a substantial amount of money on the table.

Maybe he *should* be worrying about his pack's ability to plan well enough to get him out of this alive.

His instincts told him to run, but he knew that was the quickest way to die. He couldn't outrun a shifter, and when he glanced around the parking lot, he found it empty. That wasn't likely to last if someone had heard the gunshot and called the cops.

"Well?" Reaper demanded.

"They traded him for the shifter," Tweedledee said. The muzzle of his gun was pressed into Reaper's stomach, but he didn't pull the trigger.

"Who?"

"Savino."

"Max Savino?" Reaper asked with a low chuckle. "They wouldn't let a healer go without a fight." He stepped back and turned to eye Toua like he was an interesting specimen trapped in a cage. Then he glanced into the distance with a scowl. "Let's go," he snarled, hefting Tweedledum off the ground and dragging him to the trunk. When no one moved, he bared his teeth with a low growl. "Get in the fucking car!"

Tweedledee sneered as the faint sound of sirens became audible in the distance. He shoved Toua towards the back seat before popping the trunk.

Toua slid into the back as Dante climbed in beside him. He glanced back in time to see a pair of legs disappear into the trunk before Reaper slammed it shut. The shifter stalked around the car to climb into the passenger seat, and they pulled out of the parking lot as cops were pulling onto the street.

No one spoke until they reached the highway; then Reaper turned to look at Toua and dread sank like a heavy weight in his gut. "When do they plan to come for you?"

"They didn't say." Caius had only mentioned gathering forces, but Toua hoped they'd move sooner rather than later.

Reaper narrowed his eyes and leaned over between the seats. He moved too fast to follow as he grabbed the front of Toua's hoodie and yanked him forward. "You're going to tell me everything you know," he growled, releasing his grip only to quickly squeeze his fingers around Toua's throat instead. "Or I'll kill the human and take you for myself."

Toua clawed at Reaper's hand, fighting the panic and fear as he struggled to breathe. The warm burst of magic from the ring on his finger gave him hope, but before he could activate the protections, Yaj crawled out of his hiding place in Toua's hoodie pocket with a bark of warning and raced up his arm. A moment later Reaper jerked his hand away with a snarl, Yaj hanging from his finger where he'd sunk his teeth in.

"No!" Toua shouted as Reaper flung his hand against the driver's seat hard enough to kill a small dog, but Yaj vanished with a squeak before he hit.

"Where the fuck is it?" Reaper snarled, checking his body like he expected Yaj to still be on him.

Toua sensed the sugar glider nearby thanks to the familiar bond, but so long as he was out of Reaper's grasp, he wasn't going to try too hard to find him. He rubbed his bruised throat, though he didn't dare try to heal himself. Even if he'd had his tools or food as offering, he couldn't risk setting off Dante's bomb. When he glanced at Dante, his focus was on his cupped hands, where a small tuft of white fur was poking from between his thumbs.

Toua was thankful the shifter's glare wasn't directed at him anymore, though the reprieve was short-lived when Reaper snarled and turned on him again. He pressed himself as far against the seat and door as he could.

"When and how many?" Reaper demanded.

"They didn't say. I was only with them for a couple of days."

"Who the fuck are you?" Tweedledee finally yelled.

Reaper sneered. "I work for the Order."

"We have no problems with the Order."

"I'm here for the red-eyed mage," he said, focusing on Toua again. "And you're going to bring him to me earlier than planned."

CHAPTER 18

RÍAN STALKED into the backyard to adjust the wards and allow Akito the ability to open doorways onto the property. He might have taken longer than necessary, but he needed the space to breathe and think. He'd nearly called Caius out on not taking this seriously enough a few times already, sure that if it was Max who'd been taken, every shifter in there would have been geared up and demanding he open a doorway to his location within the hour, even if it was to a moving car.

He hated the helplessness eating away at him. Maybe if he'd still had a proper mage bag, he could have rigged something to get the collar off Dante without anyone getting hurt.

He checked his phone for the hundredth time and wasn't sure if he was more relieved or worried that it showed Toua moving along the highway. At least in a car he was relatively safe from retaliation.

He crouched and pressed the heels of his hands into his eyes with a vicious "Fuck!"

The door slid open behind him, and Max and Akito stepped onto the patio. Rían pulled himself back together and stood. "Did they come up with a plan?"

Akito rolled his eyes and settled on the bench swing, stretching his arms along the back. "So far their plan is to take the whole pack in the middle of the night and swarm the place like a fucking dark ops mission."

"You don't think that'll work?"

"I'd rather blow something up."

"Me too," said Max.

Rían pinched the bridge of his nose. "Fates help me, the world doesn't need two of you."

"Hey," Akito protested, but Rían raised an unimpressed eyebrow.

"Name one time you didn't cause significant collateral damage."

"If the bastards wanted something done quick and quiet, they sent you," Akito replied with a dismissive flick of his fingers. "Not all of us are so talented as the great and fearless Red."

Max sank down onto the other side of the bench and hunched forward with his arms crossed over his knees. "What's the point in being a mage if we can't even save someone?" he muttered.

"Well, at least with Magesoul about to go under, our jobs will be a little easier in the future," Akito said dryly.

Rían snorted. "If it doesn't collapse the economy first."

Max glanced up with a frown. "Was the collar made by Magesoul?"

"Most mage tech is."

Max made a soft humming sound that Rían found suspicious. "So someone like Rena Schulz might have a way to bypass the remote?"

Akito eyed him with an incredulous laugh. "What, you just happen to have the number for the missing owner of Magesoul?"

"Not exactly," he said, standing and heading inside.

Rían propped himself against the railing as he watched Max walk up to Caius and lean into him for a kiss.

"What are you doing here, Red?"

"What do you mean?"

Akito let out an exaggerated sigh. "You had plans for a craft shop or whatever," he said, pausing for a beat for Rían to correct him.

Rían didn't bother. Experience had taught him not to indulge Akito whenever possible.

"How'd you end up here?"

When Max turned to head back towards them, Rían glanced at Akito. "Reaper was waiting for me on my last mission."

Akito gave him a dubious once-over. "You're still breathing, and you're not mangled."

"Not anymore. I was lucky." Thankfully he was saved from explaining when Max returned with Caius' phone. He retook his seat on the swing and scrolled through the contacts before calling one and putting it on speaker.

It rang out twice before a female voice answered with a sharp "What?"

"Ghost?"

"Well, if it isn't the little firestarter. What do you want?"

"Do you still have Rena?"

"Why?"

Max made a face at the phone and ignored the way Akito was staring at him like he'd grown three extra heads. "There's a collar with a bomb made by Magesoul, and I was hoping she'd know how to deactivate it."

Ghost chuckled. "So you want a favor."

"Not if you're going to want something outrageous in return."

"Outrageous is subjective," she replied, voice faint like she'd turned away from the phone.

"Outrageous to me," Max said firmly.

Ghost *tsk*ed. "You'd have never survived the Order," she muttered before the line went silent like it'd been muted.

Max frowned and glanced at Rían, who could only shrug. He'd met Ghost all of twice when he'd been loaned out to the military.

Akito leaned forward and pointed at the phone with a *what the fuck is wrong with you?* expression, which Max ignored.

When Ghost came back there was the faint sound of sobbing in the background. "The collars are made to be attuned to whatever mage uses them. There might be a kill switch somewhere, but it'd either be in the IT or R&D department," she said, sounding bored. "Is that all?"

"Thanks for nothing," Max said and hung up. He glanced up and blinked when he found both Rían and Akito eyeing him. "What?"

"'What' he asks," Akito mocked. "You're more touched in the head than Red."

Max scowled at him before turning to Rían. "Now what?"

Rían checked the tracker again and refused to let the black pit of helplessness eat him alive. If they had to wait until Toua reached California to make a move, the least they could do was be prepared. "Help me make protective amulets for everyone."

Akito tipped his head back and groaned. "You and your amulets."

"Do you have a better idea?"

"Nope," Akito said, raising his hands in defense. "I'm just here to make things go boom. And to get away from the horde of howling wolf toddlers."

Max flipped the phone over and over between his hands. "Why don't we sneak in and find the remote ourselves?"

"Walk into a drug cartel's home and hope they don't shoot us in the head?" Akito replied with a laugh. "That's fine with me, so long as you're both ready to kill them all when they see us."

Rían wouldn't admit it, but he was relieved when Max's aura flared with unease and more than a little hesitation.

"There has to be something we can do."

"Have an actual plan," Rían said and ignored Akito's smirk. "Going off on our own is likely to make things worse," he added, though it pained him to say it. They were in this mess because there were no good options, and the only way to possibly save everyone was to take risks. But he hated that it'd been Toua. He should have offered himself instead. He might not be a healer, but he could make a decent healing potion. And it might have led Reaper away from here, though with his luck, Reaper would have killed everyone including Dante and it would have all been for naught.

He scrubbed a hand over his face and pushed off the railing. "Amulets," he said. "And I might be able to cobble together some disorienting bombs."

CHAPTER 19

TOUA'S STOMACH twisted into knots when the familiar circle drive and brown stucco house came into view. They'd driven straight through the night, speeding down the highway and somehow avoiding being pulled over. He'd untangled the rope around his wrists hours ago and had been tying and untying it to keep himself calm. It was soft and silky, and he wondered if Quinn would want it back. It looked expensive.

He might have considered hooking it around Tweedledee's neck a few times, but it wouldn't have helped. If anything, it would have only ensured Reaper claimed Toua for himself. If it kept the bastard away from Rían it might be worth it, but he was choosing to put his faith in his pack and trust they'd find a way to get him out of this mess.

With a flicker of magic Yaj returned to him, and he felt the sugar glider settling in his hoodie pocket as the car came to a stop in front of the house. He shoved the small bundle of rope in with Yaj as Tweedledee climbed out and yanked Toua's door open.

"Get the fuck out," Tweedledee snapped, not giving Toua a chance to get out on his own before reaching in and dragging him out.

Toua stumbled but kept his feet, nearly going to his knees when the asshole shoved him towards the front door. As soon as they were inside, he was pushed up the stairs to Hugo's room. The moment he stepped inside, he knew it was too late. The cancer had always been aggressive, but with Toua's daily healing, it had been manageable. With his absence the last few months, the disease had spread unchecked. Even from the door Toua knew he'd never be able to heal it enough to make any significant improvement. Not without sacrificing his own health, or more likely his life.

Not that he wouldn't at least pretend to try. He wasn't stupid.

But Reaper took that choice away from him when he stalked into the room and laughed. "Looks like you're too late. I doubt he's going to live past tonight."

Tweedledee tightened his grip on Toua's arm and dragged him to the bed where Hugo was a withered, unresponsive husk. "Is he right?"

"He could live longer," Toua hedged, ignoring Reaper's derisive snort.

Tweedledee glanced at the bed with a grimace of disgust and abruptly released Toua. "I did my job. I'm done."

Toua blinked at the unexpected change. He'd been sure he would be shot and tossed out in the back garden as fertilizer. That was almost preferable to being stuck alone in a room with a soon-to-be corpse and Reaper.

"According to the Order, your contract belongs to Hugo," Reaper said, pulling a long, thin dagger from his boot. "So the moment he dies, you're free to claim."

Toua bolted for the door, but it was no use. He barely made it four steps before he was yanked back and down. Air slammed out of his lungs as he hit the floor hard enough he swore he felt something crack. He choked as he instinctively rolled to his side, trying to draw a breath, but Reaper kicked him and planted a foot on his chest, squeezing out what little air was left in Toua's lungs.

"Now, be a good little mage, and I might let your friends live when they come for you."

That was a lie, and Toua knew it. Reaper would kill everyone he could to ensure none of them came for Toua, or Rían if he managed to get hold of him too. "Fuck you," he wheezed. He pressed his thumb against his ring and activated the protection spells, and a gentle warmth wrapped around his body.

Reaper waved the bloody dagger in Toua's face. "I'd kill you now, but unclaimed healers are so hard to find." He grabbed the front of Toua's hoodie and hauled him to his feet, only to slam him into the nearest wall, and he clawed at Reaper's hand when it wrapped around his neck before realizing he could still breathe thanks to the ring. "Maybe I should kill you anyway and give your head to Rían."

Yaj raced up Toua's arm with an angry bark and bit Reaper's hand. Before he could retaliate, Yaj vanished, taking Toua with him.

The world tipped out of balance, his body stretching and condensing in a way that made him nauseous. An eternal moment later, he was on his hands and knees, dry heaving on a white carpet. "What," he rasped, "the fuck."

Yaj chirped in his ear, and Toua lifted his head to see he was in an office. Hugo's office, he suspected. He picked himself up using the edge of the desk as he heard Reaper snarling upstairs, followed by people running up the stairs. "Fuck," he hissed. He didn't have much time before hell broke loose, and he didn't want to be around when the rest of the cartel found out their boss was dead.

He needed a weapon. Not that he expected anything to work on Reaper if being shot point blank didn't even faze him. He opened the drawers anyway, hoping he'd find something. Papers, envelope opener, a stash of weed, scissors that Toua set on the desk. Another drawer had pens, batteries, and a Fleshlight, and he quickly slammed it shut. The bottom drawer had a small remote on top that caught his attention because of the faint touch of magic wrapped around it.

He picked it up and squinted at the buttons. There were only a few, marked A, DA, and a Power button. He prayed to his dragon spirit and all his ancestors that he didn't cause an explosion as he hit the Power button.

Nothing immediately blew up, and no one started screaming, so he counted it as a win. He shoved it in his pocket anyway and grabbed the scissors as the door to the office banged open.

Reaper took a few menacing steps inside, the dagger in his hand glistening with more blood than it had earlier, but Toua found he had no sympathy for the assholes who'd held him hostage for years.

A howl went up somewhere on the second floor, and Toua hoped it was Dante, free of his collar. That was about the only help Toua could expect at the moment.

Reaper snarled and took another step closer, though he stopped and glanced at the window when more howls echoed outside. "Your friends are here," he said, his lips twisting in a mockery of a smile. "I should toss them your head as a welcome gift."

Toua tightened his grip on the scissors, ready to do what little damage he could, but Yaj barked, and that nauseating, world-turning-upside-down sensation came over him again.

He landed on his back with a choked wheeze, blinking lights from his eyes before realizing they were actual lights dangling above him. "Gonna have to work on this teleporting thing," he groaned as he slowly got to his feet. This time he was in what looked like the basement. There were no windows, but he could hear people yelling upstairs. Screaming interspersed with gunshots and howls. He needed to get up there and let his pack know he was fine before any of them got killed.

He crept up the stairs, the old wood creaking with each step, but they held steady. When he reached the door, he found it locked.

"No, no, no," he whispered, breathing through the spike of fear and adrenaline as he threw his shoulder against the door. It didn't budge, and he only succeeded in bruising himself. "Fuck!" He moved back enough to drop the scissors on the top step and gripped the handrails on either side of the stairs for balance. Then he kicked the door with both feet instead. It rattled in place but held. Even after what he was sure was at least twenty minutes of kicking and ramming his shoulder into it, the door remained in place.

Toua hunched forward and braced his hands on his legs to catch his breath. "Can you not," he panted, "teleport us outside?"

Yaj offered a sad squeak, and Toua groaned as he lightly banged his head against the door. He dropped to the ground when he heard gunshots from the other side, expecting to get hit with a storm of bullets, but nothing rained down on him.

A thud followed a moment later, and he took the chance to bang on the door while praying it wasn't Reaper. "Help!" He slammed his fist against the door a few more times before pressing his ear to it to listen.

He didn't hear much at all until something rustled on the other side and someone called, "Toua?" The voice was vaguely familiar, though he couldn't put a name to it. But it wasn't Reaper and didn't sound like any of the cartel.

"Yeah," he said, his voice and body both shaky with relief. "I'm locked in."

"Get back."

Toua backed up several steps down the stairs and gripped the railing as he waited. He heard a brief conversation, and then someone smashed through the door, filling the air with splintered wood. The door didn't swing open so much as fall off and tumble down the stairs.

Toua blinked at the mage he hadn't seen in years. "Akito?"

"Aww, you remember me." Akito wiggled his fingers in greeting before pointing past Toua. "Why the fuck are you locked in the basement?"

LUKAS BREATHED deep as he watched Max's flames spread around the perimeter, catching the scent of about two dozen humans inside, with Rían reeking of tense, agitated nerves beside him. The few guards who'd been on watch were already taken care of, courtesy of Rían's disorienting bombs, and with their additional forces they should have the advantage. All that was left was ensuring no one could get away while they retrieved Toua and Dante. Then an unknown howl went up from inside, followed by screams and gunshots, and they moved into action.

Howls from Caius' pack echoed around Lukas as he kicked in the back door. The tang of fresh blood wisped through the air, but Lukas was more focused on Toua's scent, though it somehow seemed to come from above and below at once. When he turned to tell Rían to stay close, he found the mage already making his way to the stairs, one hand in his bag and the other throwing blinding white orbs at anyone who came towards him.

Muttering curses under his breath, Lukas followed, ignoring the breaking of windows and scattered howls as the rest of the pack found other ways into the house to divide and conquer. He was used to Rían's heedlessness—the mage put far too much faith in his bag and instincts for his own good—but there was a stark difference between an expanse of wilderness and the small confines of a house filled with the enemy.

"Squirrel," he hissed as he caught up to Rían at the top of the stairs. "You're going to get one of us shot."

"Their bullets don't have aconite," Rían replied, as if that was a valid excuse for Lukas to take a bullet.

A door slammed down the hall, and they both turned, though the sudden spike of fear sweat on Rían had Lukas' hackles rising even though it disappeared beneath a pulse of magic a moment later. He lifted his gun and trained it on the man who'd stopped at the end of the hall to stare at them, the grin spreading his lips making his burned face look even more deranged. A shifter, though he smelled off.

Like the acrid stench when mages started throwing dozens of spells. Reaper, he assumed, though how the bastard was here was almost as concerning as the blood dripping from his dagger.

"There you are." Reaper pointed the tip of his dagger at Rían with an accusatory *tsk*. "You're almost more trouble than you're worth."

"Glad to be of service."

Lukas didn't have the patience for their repartee. He fired three times into Reaper's chest and hoped it'd be enough to slow him down. They should have used their aconite supply, but the only shifter they'd expected to be here was Dante. "Get out," he hissed, shoving Rían back towards the stairs as Rían threw one of his bombs.

The smoke hadn't even started to clear before Reaper surged forward with enough speed and force to throw Lukas through the wall. He broke through a solid wooden beam before landing hard on his back, where his lungs tried to escape through his throat. There was no chance to process how Reaper was that strong before the bastard was on him, and Lukas barely deflected the dagger before it could sink into his chest.

Reaper latched a hand around Lukas' throat instead. "He's mine."

Lukas sneered and twisted his lower body. He managed to hook a leg around Reaper's shoulders, but throwing him off was harder than it should have been. Even off-balance Reaper maintained a bruising grip. He unleashed his wolf enough to shift his face and hands and for a bit more strength to flood his body. Sharp claws pierced Reaper's arm as Lukas grabbed on, the sharp smell of fresh blood filling his nose.

He jerked at Reaper's arm with enough force it should have broken, but Reaper barely budged and leaned down with a dark chuckle. Whatever he was going to say, he didn't get the chance.

Rían slammed part of the broken beam across the back of Reaper's head. That was finally enough that he tilted sideways, and Lukas took advantage to shove him the rest of the way off before rolling to his feet.

He emptied the rest of his clip into Reaper's back as he grabbed Rían's arm, then holstered it as he bolted from the room. He used his freed hand to activate his earpiece with a gritted out, "Reaper's here." They made it to the bottom of the stairs in time to see Leon in his gray wolf form take a few gunshots to the side before his massive jaws clamped down on the offending cartel member's thigh.

Screaming followed them, but Lukas was more concerned with getting Rían out of the house. He'd known this was a bad idea. They should have left Rían back home with Caleb regardless of the extra firepower. One trained mage was usually enough in his experience. Two plus Max was asking for complications.

Splintered wood rained down on them as Reaper bypassed the stairs and broke through the railing instead. He landed in a crouch in front of them, and when Lukas spun to find another path, a mage doorway appeared to block their way.

"Fuck," he snarled as Rían muttered one of his own curses. He shoved Rían back towards the stairs. They could jump out a window if they had to. Except another doorway shimmered into existence at the landing. He glanced to the side as he grabbed Rían by the back of his shirt, judging the distance and force he'd need to toss Rían clear of the banister.

"Don't you da—" Lukas didn't give him time to finish the threat that was sure to follow. A moment later Rían was flying through the air with an offended, "Wolf!"

Lukas braced to follow, but Reaper slammed into his side as he was pushing off. His gear dulled some of the ache from the edges of the stairs digging into him, but it couldn't do much for the sharp teeth and claws trying to gouge his face off. Even emptying his spare gun into Reaper's stomach didn't slow him.

Glass shattered against Reaper's back, and the air became unbearably cold. Lukas' lungs shriveled up tighter than his nuts in a freezing lake. He had a quick moment of crystal-clear sight of Reaper's shoulder and neck seeming to frost over before he shoved the bastard down the stairs. Drawing breath was still a challenge, but breathing was overrated compared to not being mauled to death, so he staggered to his feet, climbed onto the railing, and launched himself at the banister half a story above him.

He missed the handrail but snagged a baluster and hauled himself over. Rían pulled him to his feet, and they ran, Reaper's choked-off threats chasing them.

They tumbled into the nearest room, the stench of blood, sickness, and death stinging his nose and sitting heavy at the back of his throat. "Window," he said, hoping Max's flames were far enough away they wouldn't fall into them.

Rían snatched an empty IV stand and launched it at the window, where it sailed through another doorway instead. When they turned, Reaper stalked into the room. The frost still covering a quarter of his body filled the air around him with fog.

"I'm going to flay your skin off one layer at a time," Reaper snarled. He kicked the door shut, effectively trapping them.

Lukas swore and checked his gear as he closed the distance to Rían. Surely he had something that would do some damage. He paused as he hit a pocket he apparently hadn't cleared in months and eyed Rían as he curled his fingers around the grenade. "Kinkajou."

Rían scowled, but they didn't have a chance to sort out more details. Reaper was already moving towards them, a shiny silver orb in one hand and dagger in the other, and whatever was making him fifty times stronger than the average shifter meant they were running out of time. Trusting Rían to shield them from the blast, Lukas pulled the pin and tapped it to the bottom of the grenade to activate the spell to shorten the countdown. It blew up before he'd tossed it clear, and intense heat enveloped his fingers.

Rían's magic wrapped tight around him to block the rest, but the barrier flickered and sputtered out as quickly as it formed. Lukas barely heard the irate curses before the explosion hit him full force.

The room tumbled around him in a cacophony of shattering glass, the cracking of wood, and deafening rush of heat. He slammed into something solid with a grunt and rolled to his knees, shaking his head against the muffled ringing in his ears. When he finally got to his feet, he found the room demolished, two walls blown out, and Rían and Reaper gone.

The shimmering mage doorway was still there, and he stumbled towards it with a snarled curse. Stepping through would be a calculated risk, but one he was willing to take. They hadn't come all this way to retrieve one mage just to lose another.

Lukas rushed the doorway, hoping to at least take Reaper by surprise on the other side, but instead of going through he bounced off as if hitting a mage barrier. He hit the ground, rolled, and got back on his feet with a growl. He pressed his earpiece to ask Akito if he could break through a barrier, but all he heard was the silence of broken comms.

A faint pulse of magic preceded a black ball sailing through the doorway, where it bounced across the floor. The blinking red light and high-pitched whine were warning enough. Lukas didn't hesitate to throw himself through the obliterated wall. His feet hit the ground, and then the force of the explosion above him pushed him flat as if gravity momentarily tripled.

Debris rained down on him as he struggled to get his abused lungs to resume working again. "Fuck," he groaned, spitting dirt out of his mouth and rolling onto his side to assess the damage. The entire side and half of the house were gone, along with the room he'd been standing in. So was the mage doorway.

Shouts echoed from somewhere too far away to make out the words. He picked himself up and made his way towards them, blinking against the black spots in his wavery vision and waiting for his healing to fix whatever new damage he'd suffered.

"Anyone not staying better get their ass through the doorway now!" Akito shouted.

"Lukas!" Quinn broke away from the pack and latched on to Lukas, propping a shoulder under his arm for support. "What happened?"

"Reaper." Lukas grimaced as he glanced over the pack, his gaze skirting past Toua before he focused on Caius. "I'm sorry. He got Rían."

Toua's shock and fear were a sudden bitterness beneath the smoke and flames. "No. No! Find him!"

"We will," Caius said, even as the wail of sirens grew louder in the distance.

"He used a doorway. It wouldn't let me through," he said, looking to Akito. "Can you track where it led?"

Akito's dubious look wasn't promising, but he nodded. "I'll see what I can do. You all need to leave."

Toua refused to budge, and Lukas and Quinn had to pull him away by force. He didn't stop struggling until they were through Akito's doorway and the scenery changed to the trees of a deep forest. Then he sagged in their grips as if he couldn't hold himself up anymore, the black scent of his despair churning with the guilt building in Lukas' gut.

CHAPTER 20

RÍAN CAME to with a groan. Everything hurt, and he was cold. His throat ached, his nose burned, and his lungs refused to fill with a deep enough breath. When he finally managed to sit up, he saw why. Thick iron bars surrounded him, trapping him in a large cage. The floor was bare concrete. His shoes were missing, and the floor was cool against his palms.

"What the fuck," he croaked, his vision spinning as he pushed onto his knees. Panic beat a steady rhythm beneath his heartbeat, but he was too disoriented for it to take hold yet. He pressed a hand to a throbbing ache on the back of his head and his fingers came away tacky with drying blood. He didn't remember getting hit. He remembered rushing into the house with Lukas, desperate to find Toua. Shouting and howls and gunfire. Reaper. An explosion he'd shielded against. Tried to shield? And then... nothing.

"Niamh," he whispered, the panic fluttering faster when there was no response. He checked his pockets with sluggish movements, and then the hood of his hoodie, but there was no tiny furry warmth hidden in them. "Niamh," he tried again, louder, choking on the dust and taste of iron.

He turned at the sound of a small scuffle, and Niamh raced to him from the shadows between the cage and the wall. "There you are," he breathed, scooping her into his hand. He didn't sense any injury, but that was a small comfort when he was trapped in a cage. Especially when he reached for his magic and it failed to answer him, as if it were being suppressed.

His bag was conveniently missing, but as he regained enough sense to take in his own condition, he found most of his amulets still attached and functional thanks to Max's magic. Their power was already partially drained, so someone had tried to remove them, but they were intact enough to ease some of the panic.

As his eyes adjusted to the dim light, he saw more cages stretched out on either side of and across from him. The panic returned a hundredfold when he saw someone in each of them.

"No...." He struggled to his feet and stepped as close to the bars as he could, staring across the short distance to the next cage and squinting into the gloom. The person there looked familiar, like a professor's assistant who'd gone missing last year. "Aliyah?"

The hunched figure stirred and lifted her head to look at him. "Rían?" She shifted closer, pushing grimy, tangled hair away from her face. "He got you too?"

His breaths stuck in his lungs. His mind had fought against connecting those dots, and hearing it confirmed was a punch to the gut. He reached for the bars to steady himself and pulled away with a soft snarl when his skin began itching. "He took you?"

Aliyah's lips quirked into a faint miserable smile. "He took all of us. Anyone who spoke out against the Order or who weren't worth the trouble of keeping bound."

Rían glanced at the countless cages around them. The walls were the same concrete as the floor, and the pressure of dank air suggested they were underground. The room wasn't small; it had the feeling of a cave. "How many?" he asked softly.

"I don't know. Less than a hundred."

Before he could ask more, a door opened and light spilled in from the top of some stairs about two rows over. Even from that distance he recognized Reaper. He quickly twisted a ring off his finger, the one he'd taken back from Toua that shielded the wearer from tracking or detection, and slipped it over Niamh's tail. She barked softly in protest, but he reached back to set her by the bars.

"Go," he ordered. "Only come back if you can't get out."

She let out a soft angry chirp, but as Reaper started down the stairs, she turned and vanished into the shadows.

Rían had no doubt Reaper was coming for him, so he sat in the middle of the cage with his legs crossed and waited. The slow, deliberate footsteps ratcheted up his nerves, but he breathed through it even as he heard those in the cages around him shifting to press themselves into the back corners.

Panic was his worst enemy right then, and he refused to give in to it. He was alive, relatively unharmed, and he wasn't bound. He might have been cut off from his magic with no chance of calling his Sidhe in an iron cage, but he wasn't powerless. Reaper wanted him for something, even if it was a binding.

When the footsteps drew closer, he closed his eyes as if meditating, focusing on his breaths and struggling to slow his rapid heartbeat.

Reaper stopped in front of his cage and stood there in silence, but Rían did his best to ignore him.

If it was a battle of will, he could play. He might not have the patience and experience of Lukas when it came to lying in wait, but he had plenty of experience with spite.

The minutes ticked by until his legs started going tingly, but a bit of poor blood circulation was nothing compared to outwaiting the fucking Reaper.

Plus, the longer Reaper focused on him, the better a chance Niamh would have to escape.

Something tapped against the iron bars, and he tensed, listening for something to open and give him a chance to fight, but there was only a slow, steady tapping like a nail scraping against the bar. The continuous sound did nothing for his nerves, but he refused to react. Denying Reaper any response was the only power he had right then, and he wasn't going to give that up until he was forced to.

He counted the taps and reached 174 before they stopped. The silence that followed was as disorienting as waking up in the cell to begin with. Then the footsteps returned and walked away.

Rían kept his eyes closed, sure it wouldn't be over so quick or easy. Only when he heard a cage door creak open down the row did his breathing stutter, and he started to open his eyes. He caught himself before he could look, digging his nails into his thighs as Reaper dragged a mage from their cage and hauled them upstairs.

When the door slammed shut, Rían slumped forward and pressed his fists into his eyes until he saw sparks of color.

"He'll come back tomorrow," Aliyah whispered.

"Great," he muttered, which earned a coughing laugh. He lifted his head with a frown and turned to her. "How is he doing this? Keeping everyone fed and our magic suppressed."

"Stasis spells," she replied with a soft snarl. "Lots of them. Someone from the Order comes around every few months to refresh them."

"Who?" he demanded, but she shook her head.

"They wear a cloak and never get close enough to see them."

Rían stood and limped around the boundary of his cage as his legs regained feeling. Obviously the Order knew about this. Even if Reaper was known as their assassin, the Order would verify the kills. Or ensure their disappearances were permanent. "He put bindings on all of you?"

"Most of us."

He hated to ask, but he had to. "And your familiars?"

Aliyah's breath caught on an aborted sob. "Dead."

Rían closed his eyes and breathed, instinctively reaching for his familiar bond with Niamh. It was still there, as strong and solid as ever, and while he couldn't tell if she'd found a way to free herself yet, he didn't sense that she was in danger. Losing a familiar bond wasn't fatal, but he'd heard it was like losing a limb. Something that was an integral part of a mage and a pillar for their magical control. Mages usually found their familiars shortly after Sparking, but with the Order taking possession of them as soon as possible, sometimes familiars weren't found until mages began leaving the castle on missions.

He'd found Niamh and her siblings on his first solo mission, when Australian wildfires had gotten out of control and mages were called in to help. He wouldn't let Reaper kill her. He wouldn't let the bastard kill him either.

He wasn't sure how, but he would get out of here.

He'd get all of them out of here.

CHAPTER 21

THREE DAYS.

Three days and not a single sign of Rían.

Akito had tried scrying for him, an old spell-casting technique that had been hit or miss even before the advent of technology, and found nothing.

Toua struggled to believe Rían was even still alive if Reaper had gotten hold of him. As much as he hoped Rían was still breathing, he had to wonder if death wouldn't be a better fate.

A few members of Caius' pack came and went throughout the days, but Caleb, Dante, and Akito more or less moved into the packhouse, and the bedroom furniture he'd ordered suited them fine.

Toua didn't pay much attention to them after healing them. He didn't pay much attention to anyone. He put together the altar he'd ordered and set it in the back corner of the living room, then spent hours every day praying to his spirit companion and his ancestors for any sign or guidance to finding Rían.

They weren't exactly silent, but he got nothing useful from them either. He went through each day more numb than the last, occasionally drowning in guilt. If he hadn't agreed to the trade to begin with, maybe Reaper wouldn't have had the chance to ambush them. He picked up several pieces of spirit paper and centered his thoughts, focusing on his ancestors and the good spirits around him as he begged them to protect Rían, wherever he was.

RÍAN LOST track of time.

He counted days by the number of times Reaper came to stand in front of his cage, but with the stasis spells, even that gave him doubt. Sometimes it seemed like hours between one visit and the next, others like days.

No one spoke much. Aliyah did sometimes, answering what questions he dared to ask. She'd been missing for almost a year, but she swore it felt longer. Every other mage near him looked defeated and ignored him rather than respond to him, but Rían refused to give up.

When Reaper wasn't terrorizing them by banging on their bars with a metal bat, Rían was walking the perimeter of his cage. Barely six steps on each side, and there was nothing inside. He couldn't touch the iron for long, but that didn't keep him from throwing himself against every bar, testing for any weakness. Despair clawed through his chest until it was ravaged to shreds, but he kept moving. He couldn't stop or give in or he'd break, and that was what Reaper was waiting for.

It would happen eventually. Days, weeks, months, years. He hoped he wouldn't be trapped that long, but Reaper obviously had the Order's support. No one was going to find him. Not without help.

The fact Niamh hadn't returned gave him some hope. The familiar bond was still there, growing fainter every day, but a sugar glider, even a familiar, could only travel so far. If he was lucky, he was somewhere in the States. If he was overseas, it'd be years before Niamh made her way back to her siblings, if she even could.

One of the worst things about the stasis spells was never being hungry or thirsty or tired enough to sleep. No bodily requirements to give any indication of time passing. Stuck fully awake and aware, able to hear the shuffling of others in cages around him. The slow drip of water into a puddle somewhere nearby. The low hum of something kicking on and off above them, likely the heat or AC.

Every time panic threatened to spike his adrenaline, he stopped pacing and closed his eyes and quietly counted to fifty in every language he knew, until the hoarse whisper of his voice dragged him into a meditative state. Then he repeated the mantra that was helping him keep a grip on his sanity.

Tá mé ceart go leor.

Over and over and over again.

I'm fine, I'm fine, I'm fine, I'm fine….

WHEN REAPER showed up again, he set a bucket outside Rían's cage and tipped it over, spilling cold water across the floor.

Rían's heart rate sped up, but he remained where he was seated in the middle of the cage. He had nowhere to run to, and defying Reaper like this was a habit after so many times now. A ritual he had to cling to until he couldn't anymore.

Reaper walked away, his heavy boots echoing against the concrete as he moved farther down the row and opened a cage. Rían cracked his eyes open as Reaper pulled a middle-aged man out of one cage and a woman from another before dragging them both down to Rían's.

The woman didn't look familiar, but the man did. A dream mage who'd vanished several years ago. One of the only ones seen this century.

Foreboding twisted in his gut. Dream mages could be fearsome, but their powers only worked on someone who was sleeping. Or rather, unconscious. His suspicions were confirmed when Reaper shoved the woman to her knees.

"Do it," he ordered.

Rían's lungs constricted. *This isn't real. It's not real, not real.*

She didn't look at Rían as she reached out and touched her fingers to the wet concrete. Silver arcs of lightning raced across the floor and multiplied tenfold when they bounced off the iron bars.

Rían's amulets activated, but he knew they wouldn't last long against a sustained onslaught. It only took a few minutes for the protective magic to fizzle out, and by then the entire cage was lit up with blinding streaks of lightning. Silver clouded his vision before one of the crackling bolts slammed into his chest, his entire body seizing with the force of raw electricity coursing through him.

The dream mage's eyes lit up with a pale blue glow that somehow looked brighter than the lightning.

That was the last thing he saw before his vision went dark, his mantras still echoing in his mind.

I'm fine, it's not real. I'm fine, it's not real, not real, not real.

CHAPTER 22

RÍAN WOKE on his side, choking and gasping for air. He was damp from the spilled water, and Reaper and both mages were still in front of the cage. He couldn't have been unconscious long, even though his body was stiff and sore as if he hadn't moved in a day.

It took forever to push himself up and for his lungs to start working properly, and the moment he did, Reaper opened the door of his cage.

Rían didn't have the strength or presence of mind to try to get up and out or defend himself. Unforgiving fingers gripped his face as Reaper leaned in close.

"You belong to me," he snarled.

"Fuck you," Rían slurred, shoving at Reaper's chest, but it was like pushing against an iron wall.

Reaper smirked and shoved Rían down to pin him against the floor. His shirt tore when Reaper roughly jerked it away enough to bare Rían's neck and then sharp teeth broke his skin.

A hoarse scream ripped out of Rían's throat as pain clawed through his neck and shoulder.

He didn't remember passing out, but he blinked his eyes open and found he was alone. He curled in on himself, pressing his hands against his eyes before tentatively sliding a hand to his neck. It stung beneath his touch, the flesh swollen around a bite mark, and his fingers came away smeared with blood.

"Tá mé ceart go leor," he whispered. He was fine. A claim wouldn't last on him. It couldn't. And even if it did, a shifter claim wasn't a binding. It might make Reaper stronger with the feedback of power, but Rían refused to be controlled by it.

He tugged his torn shirt tighter around himself and pulled his knees to his chest. He knew he couldn't give in, but what was the point? He was sure it'd been weeks. Possibly months. If Lukas' pack hadn't found him by now they likely never would. And Niamh might not ever make it back to them. She was still alive, but for how long? She'd never survived more than a day on her own since Rían rescued the three of them. It was a miracle she'd made it as long as she had.

He lost track of time even more as he stayed where he was. The stasis spells kept him from developing new aches from lying on the floor, and he tried to let his mind go blank. To distance himself from the fact he was trapped in a living nightmare.

He tried to let go and imagine he was back in the packhouse, training Max or antagonizing Lukas or sleeping next to Toua. Or kissing Toua. He should have kissed him when he'd had the chance, except then this situation would be even worse for both of them.

He could imagine it, though. Hot breaths on his cheek. Soft lips on his. Fingers in his hair and warm skin beneath his own. It was almost too painful to hold on to the hope of ever seeing any of them again. Some of the mages had been here for years. Maybe those on the other side had been here decades. No one went searching for mages when they vanished. The Order either listed them as KIA or conveniently lost all records of their existence.

No one was coming for him. He wasn't pack like Toua. They had no obligation to search for him.

Before he could spiral further, the door banged open and Reaper came down the stairs. He walked across the room like he had all the time in the world and stopped in front of Rían's cage. "Get up," he ordered.

Rían ignored him but found his body moving anyway, which shouldn't have been possible. Not unless Reaper had put a binding on him, but he didn't sense one. Only the ache in his shoulder from the claiming bite. He bared his teeth as he moved to stand in front of the bars. "One of these days I'm going to kill you."

Reaper grinned at him. "You're welcome to try," he said as he pushed the cage door in.

Rían's breath stuttered when the iron brushed against his hand and arm as it swung past.

"Follow," Reaper ordered before turning for the stairs.

His body moved on its own, but there was no pull of a compulsion. Nothing that suggested a binding was controlling him. He reached his hand out and let his fingers drag across the iron bars of the cages he passed, focusing on the rough edges and imperfections in the metal as he silenced the louder screams of his instincts and tuned out the way his heart beat out a rhythm of *not real, not real, not real.*

UPSTAIRS WAS more concrete and another set of stairs that led into an extravagant house. Bright afternoon light spilled across light hardwood flooring through floor-to-ceiling windows. The furniture was sleek leather, and the kitchen was filled with stainless steel. On the other side of the windows was nothing but desert. Brown dirt and rocks, giant cacti, and a large tree with spiky branches.

For all his traveling, Rían had rarely been sent into the deserts, but he was fairly certain this was the Mojave. He wasn't trapped somewhere overseas. He was still a long way from Denver, but maybe, just maybe, Niamh would make it home.

Home?

He wasn't sure he could call it home. He hadn't had a home in over a decade, but maybe, if he ever got free from here....

"Tell me your specialty," Reaper demanded, appearing in front of Rían.

He waited for the strange spells to force him to talk, but nothing happened. He restrained his smirk, but he'd take any control he could get in whatever was going on.

Reaper stepped closer until they were nose to nose. "Answer."

Rían spit in his face and didn't regret it even when Reaper punched him in return.

It hadn't felt hard enough to knock him out, but after the burst of pain faded he found himself back in his cage. Only now he was strapped to a chair. A bright light above him blinded him to most everything, but he sensed at least two people in front of him. One leaned in, and Reaper gripped Rían's arms where they were tied to the chair, his claws digging into Rían's flesh and drawing blood.

"You're going to tell me everything I want to know."

"Go fuck yourself."

"You're more my type."

Rían's heart rate tripled—*not real, not real, not real*—as he tried to kick Reaper away from him, but his legs were restrained like his arms.

Reaper chuckled, a dark sound that grated along Rían's spine, and stepped back. A moment later Aliyah replaced him, and Rían struggled against his restraints with a helpless snarl of frustration.

Her magic twisted around him, and drops of water coalesced around Rían's head.

His heart hammered in his chest—*notrealnotrealnotreal*—as the water condensed and he suffocated.

He squeezed his eyes shut and wished he was anywhere but here. His body could survive this; Reaper wouldn't let him die so easily. But real or not, he knew he'd break. The only way he could get through this and still be himself at the end was to lose part of himself now, and he felt the shift as something splintered inside him.

The water disappeared when his vision began to blacken and left him gasping for air, but his senses had dulled. Like he'd detached from his body. He was aware of the water closing around him again, of his body's reflexive struggle to get free. The panic beating counterpoint beneath the *not real not real not real* of his heart seemed to fade away.

When Reaper appeared in front of him again, he didn't look real. Like his face was made of plastic. He shouted something, but Rían barely understood him, and even if he'd wanted to answer, he found he couldn't speak.

That suited him just fine.

Rían closed his eyes and let the world fade away.

CHAPTER 23

LUKAS WAS going to murder someone.

Over a week with no sign or trace of Rían was unacceptable, though he knew everyone was doing everything they could.

Caius had called every contact he had in the armed forces who might know anything about Reaper, but as the Order's private assassin, he may as well not even exist. The only rumor to surface came from Caius' ex, Charlie, when she got her hands on some classified intel: Reaper had a home in Nevada, but that was unverified, and even its general rumored location was unknown.

As soon as the police were done sniffing around the cartel house, Akito took several members of the Wyoming pack out every day, where they moved in ever-widening circles that focused on moving closer to Nevada. He'd had no luck tracing where the doorway had connected to, something that could apparently only be done so long as the other end of the connection wasn't shielded.

Quinn had set up so many new scrubbers and searches on the deep and dark webs that their electricity bill was likely going to be insane. Max coordinated the searches with Akito to make sure they were always covering new ground, but his scent alternated between frustrated and hopeless.

Caleb and Dante kept to themselves as much as possible, hiding away in their room.

Lukas couldn't exactly blame them. Even now Dante rarely spoke before touching his throat first, as if he couldn't believe the collar was gone. Two extra noses wouldn't help in the grand scheme of things anyway, especially when they were both traumatized from their time with the cartel.

And Toua....

Toua was a mess of misery, guilt, and anger. When he wasn't demanding they do more faster, he was hunched over praying in front of his altar.

For once Lukas couldn't stand the waiting. He knew who the target was, but until they found Reaper, he was useless. Stuck marinating in his own guilt and self-loathing for letting Reaper get his hands on Rían. He couldn't even reach out to his own few contacts in the armed forces without risking the unwanted attention of whoever had tried to kill him.

The sky was still dark outside as he poured himself some coffee. He desperately needed to go for a run, but so long as Reaper had his sights on Toua or Max, Caius wasn't willing to risk any of them going out alone, and Quinn and Max were burning their candles from both ends. He couldn't drag them out of what little sleep they managed just because he was restless.

He turned as he heard the soft pad of Rui's feet. The small leopard's yellow eyes glinted in the low light, but the more familiar yet still concerning sight was Toua's sugar glider playing dead in Rui's mouth, and Max's perched on top of her head. She flicked her tail at Lukas and walked towards the back door. Before he could think to open it for her, they vanished and reappeared on the patio, then continued towards the fence, where a semipermanent doorway was kept open for those going to or returning from a search.

Lukas pressed his fingers against his eyes and shook his head. If the familiars wanted to help, let them. Not like they were any use sitting around the house. With nothing to do that could possibly help find Rían, he turned his attention to the practical task of making breakfast. He and Quinn made a point to haul Toua out of the house for groceries every few days, even if Toua wasn't up for cooking much. Lukas pulled up a recipe for quiche that looked simple enough and set to work making ten of them.

Once he had two in the oven, he realized they didn't have enough pie plates for ten and resorted to tearing the premade pie crusts to cover the larger baking dishes. Then he poured the last of the egg mixture into them instead. It would be fine.

He refilled his coffee, set a timer on his phone, and then stood in the middle of the kitchen with the restless, frustrated despair that threatened to eat him alive every time he had more than ten seconds to think. Even after he washed the too-many dishes he'd used, no one else was up yet, so he moved to the back door and stared out at the trees rising above the privacy fence.

Blaming Rían for refusing to join their pack added only a little guilt and shame to the pile already suffocating him. Maybe if they'd had the pack bond to focus on, they could have found him by now.

"Where the fuck are you, squirrel?"

BY THAT afternoon Lukas was even more on edge. The pressure of constant stress and dark emotions filling the house was like drowning in still water. Something or someone would break soon, and it wouldn't be pretty.

The familiars hadn't returned. Quinn was downstairs, typing away at his computer loudly enough Lukas could hear the click of his keys. Caius was arguing with someone on the phone in his office. Max was slumped over the dining table, hands clutching his hair as he stared forlornly at the map spread out in front of him, and Toua was in the corner in some kind of trance.

Lukas was pouring his too-many-to-count refill of coffee when something changed. He spun and scanned the room. Max was still hunched in his chair, but Toua's breathing had quickened. "Toua?" he called quietly, setting his coffee aside and moving across the room.

Toua was still in a trance, whispering under his breath, but Lukas didn't speak the language.

He crouched beside Toua, unwilling to interrupt whatever was going on unless Toua started seizing or something.

"What's wrong?" Max asked, coming up behind Lukas.

"No clue, but something happened."

Max dropped a hand to Lukas' hair and combed through it, and he took it as an invitation to lean into Max's legs. He let his eyes fall partially shut as he continued watching Toua. They didn't have long to wait before he groaned and listed sideways. Lukas caught him before he hit the floor and tugged him closer to prop him against the sofa.

"Mojave," Toua whispered, his hand flailing for a moment before he found Lukas' arm and latched on. That seemed to give him focus, and he tightened his fingers as he sucked in a harsh breath. "He's in the Mojave Desert."

"How do you know?" Lukas asked as Max ran up the stairs yelling for Caius.

Toua's expression nearly shattered before he pushed away from Lukas and swayed to his feet. "His spirit told me."

LUKAS CHECKED his rifles and gear over as his pack finished prepping around him. Toua hadn't gotten much info from Rían's spirit, whatever the fuck that meant, but he said it would be easier to find him once they were in the desert.

Max and Toua had disappeared shortly after they spread the news and were currently out back with a couple of horns and a live hen and rooster. Lukas had heard the mention of a sacrifice and decided he didn't need or want to hear more.

He glanced at Quinn as he came upstairs in his tactical gear and with a sword in hand. Lukas stopped in the middle of filling the spare magazine for his AXSR and raised an eyebrow.

"What?" Quinn asked, pressing the sword to his chest with a defensive glare. "Toua gets one, why can't I?"

Akito snorted where he stood next to Lukas, flicking a lighter open and closing it over the flame in an obvious nervous tic.

"What's wrong?" Lukas asked.

Akito snapped the lighter shut and wrapped his hand around it. "Nothing," he said after a moment, and Lukas smelled the lie, but Akito continued. "Just never thought I'd be going up against Reaper."

"Hopefully this'll be the last time anyone has to deal with him," Lukas muttered. If this wasn't a trap, they had a good chance of taking care of the bastard once and for all. It didn't feel like a trap. It felt like the only chance they'd ever get of finding Rían and getting him back.

He just hoped the spirit issue didn't mean he was dead.

AN HOUR and a half later the pack and a dozen of the Wyoming shifters were circled around Toua in the middle of the desert. It would have been sooner, but for some reason they'd had to wait for Toua to cook the chickens he'd sacrificed. Lukas still didn't want to know, so he hadn't asked, though the delay was infuriating when they finally had a target in sight. Only the fact that Toua was insistent it was all necessary despite his own frustration made waiting at all tolerable.

He scanned the horizon that was empty of anything other than rocks, cacti, and the occasional tree. It was warmer than Denver but still late enough in the season that Lukas wasn't sweating. He might not believe Fenrir was a deity with much, if any, power to help the mere mortals of his descendants, but Lukas prayed for some kind of blessing regardless.

Akito had brought them as close to the center of the desert within Nevada's border as he could in hopes it would make their search faster. Toua had a strange black hood on his head that hid his face—one of his only possessions they'd been able to retrieve from the cartel house—his sword in one hand, a metal circle with small discs on it in the other, and his bag with other supplies on his arm.

Toua went into one of his trances, though this one didn't last nearly as long as his others. Within another hour they stepped through their fourth doorway, and Lukas spotted the building in the distance. Single story, floor-to-ceiling glass windows, and large enough to be considered a mansion.

Akito let out a low whistle, lifting a hand to shield his eyes against the sun. "That's definitely it. There's enough magic surrounding the area it's making my teeth vibrate."

That wasn't a good sign, though not exactly surprising. Even worse, there was no decent cover anywhere. Lukas wouldn't be able to set up a shot without being completely exposed, though the chance of Reaper setting foot outside his protections was slim.

"Can you make sure he can't open a doorway and escape?" Caius asked.

Akito laughed, though it cut short a second later. "Oh, you're serious." He cleared his throat and flicked his fingers. "Sorry, I'm not that talented or powerful."

The wind picked up with a cool breeze, and Lukas bared his teeth as he caught the scent of rain. "Did anyone check the forecast?"

"Don't bother," Akito said, his voice tight. "That's storm magic."

"Guess it's safe to say he knows we're here," Quinn said. He drew his gun and flipped the safety off as he chambered a round. The sharp tang of aconite in the bullets burned Lukas' nose.

"Max, with me," Caius said. "Akito, with Quinn. Toua, with Lukas. The rest of you, spread out and find a point of entry."

Lukas slung his AXSR rifle to his back and settled his hands around the M27 across his chest instead. He stepped up beside Toua, who was putting his black hood into his bag. "Ready?"

Toua looked up, determination hardening his expression despite the exhaustion in every line of his body. "We're getting him back."

"Damn straight," Lukas said. "Stay behind me." He took point and fell in behind the others as they made for the house. He expected some kind of attack, but other than the wind picking up enough speed to whistle and the sky darkening, there was nothing. They were still at least thirty yards out when the hair on his arms stood up. With a twist of dread in his gut, he lifted his arm and was rewarded with a low buzz of electricity around his hand.

"Take cover!" he shouted, reaching back for Toua and dragging him forward. "Run!" He kept hold of Toua to ensure he kept his feet, half carrying him as he raced for the house.

A giant flamethrower spewage of fire, courtesy of Akito, stretched out over their heads, disrupting the gathering energy long enough for them to reach the house. They plastered themselves against the sides as lightning crackled and erupted around them like the house was the center of a plasma globe. Over and over the sky cracked open and bright streaks of lightning hit the ground around them, throwing dirt and rocks and leaving charred black behind.

One struck close enough that a tiny arm broke off and struck Lukas' earpiece. He slapped it away with a hiss as the earpiece fizzled and popped in a tiny burst of fried electrics. "Fuck." He spared a glance to the others who'd made it to their side of the house to see most of them had lost their communications too.

When he turned back, Toua was trailing his fingers along the wall with a frown of concentration. "What is it?" Lukas asked.

"There's a fracture in the wards here." He took a few steps closer to the center of the wall and crouched down, seemingly unconcerned as more lightning cascaded around them and thunder threatened to shatter Lukas' eardrums. "Here." Toua pointed to a weak spot in the foundation that seemed to be crumbling.

"Step back," Lukas said, lifting his gun once Toua was out of the way and firing several rounds. Thankfully he hadn't switched them out for aconite bullets because mud, plaster, and debris ricocheted back at him. When he eased off, there was a small hole in the ground, and when he crouched for a better look, he saw it led into something like a basement.

He gave a sharp whistle, and a few of the Wyoming pack answered, using the butts of their guns and shifter strength to widen the hole enough for someone to wiggle inside. When Toua moved as if he intended to go through first, Lukas hauled him back with a soft growl. "Stay here until I clear it."

Toua glared but didn't protest.

Lukas pointed to Leon and another shifter he couldn't remember the name of. "Watch him," he said before eyeing the hole. He removed his AXSR and passed it to Leon, resisting the urge to tell him he wanted it back in one piece before he lowered himself into the basement.

He landed with a splash in a deep puddle that nearly covered the top of his boots and lowered into a crouch. He got his M27 situated and lifted it at the ready. The light was dim, but he blinked his wolf eyes into focus as he moved forward. The source of the odd smell immediately became apparent as he realized he was surrounded by cages with people in them.

"Fucking hell," he whispered, reaching the end of the aisle and turning to find they stretched for at least twenty yards in both directions. "There's at least a hundred cages in here…." He couldn't believe they were all occupied, and he didn't have the time to check as he made a quick sweep, but he had a sinking feeling most of them were.

Once he was convinced Reaper wasn't down there, he hurried back to the hole and whistled an all clear. Leon dropped down, followed by Toua, and then the other shifters. Lukas did another visual sweep while they got their bearings before heading towards the opposite wall of the way he'd already checked.

He kept catching hints of Rían's scent, but with all the bodies in here, they'd have to find him by sight.

Toua made a strangled sound and shoved past them as he hurried to a cage close to the far corner. Rían was inside, strapped to a chair. He was shirtless, and his chest was covered in burns and smears of blood. One eye was black and swollen completely shut.

Toua jerked on the iron door, but it didn't budge. Even Leon couldn't open it. It took all of them straining against it for the door to scrape open enough for anyone to get inside.

Lukas joined Toua in getting Rían free, pulling his knife from his thigh sheath to cut through the leather restraints. Toua pulled out incense and small bronze rings that jingled and had ribbons on them from his bag and seemed ready to go straight to healing. Lukas didn't think this was the time or place for that, but another rumble of thunder proved outside wasn't any safer. And then something exploded above them, and he prayed it was one of the pyros.

"Are you good here?" he asked. Other than the hole they'd come in from he could only see one door. So long as it was guarded, this was likely the safest place for now.

"Yes," Toua said tightly, glancing up at Lukas as he settled a hand on Rían's head. "Go get the bastard."

Lukas nodded and slipped out of the cage. He waited for Leon to take his place and snagged his AXSR to settle on his back again. "Help him with whatever he needs," he said before motioning for one of the other shifters to follow him to the door at the top of the stairs. "Guard this." Then he slipped through the door and quietly made his way up a second set of stairs.

He could hear the fighting more clearly as he cracked the next door open. The rapid retort of at least two guns firing, pained howls, the crackle of magic, and Quinn shouting, "Why won't you fucking die!"

Beyond the door was a sprawling living room next to a kitchen, and the large glass windows looking out on the desert. A quick glance outside showed the rain and lightning had mostly stopped, but the sky was still dark, and deep puddles of water were slowly seeping into the parched earth.

Lukas turned and followed the sounds of fighting deeper into the house. A stray crackle of condensed lightning whizzed by him as he neared a door at the back of the house. He pressed himself against the wall and risked a quick glance inside to scope the situation.

Some kind of entertainment room. A large wall-mounted TV on one side with a large sectional, and the other side set up like some kind of strip club. Max and Akito had the storm mage cornered by the sectional, while Caius, Quinn, and a few other shifters had Reaper pinned down behind the far side of the raised platform. From the looks of it, Reaper had a stash of weapons and was managing to hold everyone off.

He risked another quick look at the ceiling, but there was nothing up high enough to give him a way to set up a shot. There was a large window near Reaper, though, so he turned and hurried back to the main living area. He went outside and ran around to the back of the house, where he spotted an abandoned van rusting several yards out. The line of sight looked good as he got closer, so he set his M27 aside and hoisted himself on top of the van with his sniper rifle.

He was close enough that it didn't take long to set up. The angle wasn't perfect, he wasn't as high as he'd have liked, but he could make it work. He slowed his breathing as he focused on the shot.

Reaper was slumped behind the platform, squeezed between it and the wall, fumbling with reloading his gun. Streaks of blood and silver-blue aconite covered his face and arms, but somehow he was still moving.

Quinn's head popped up briefly on the far side of the platform, and Lukas exhaled a sharp hiss. Idiot was going to get himself killed.

He flipped the safety off and settled his finger on the trigger. The wind died down, which was a blessing. Now he just needed Reaper to sit up and away from the wall a bit more for a clean shot.

Reaper finished reloading his gun and shifted to his knees as Quinn dove into view and emptied his magazine. Reaper's body jerked with the hits, but he didn't go down, and he lifted his gun to return fire.

Lukas breathed out and pulled the trigger.

The glass shattered at the same time that Reaper fired. An echo of pain exploded in Lukas' shoulder, but he breathed through it. Even an aconite bullet wouldn't be fatal in the shoulder. Quinn would be fine.

But Reaper was still on his knees with his arm lifted, and for a moment Lukas doubted he'd made the shot. So he fired again and again, emptying all ten rounds into Reaper's head. Even though he could see the wounds healing from his spot on the van, he couldn't believe it. No one should be able to survive that. He slid off the van and grabbed his other rifle as he ran for the window, but he barely had time to clear the jagged glass stuck in the edges and take aim before Quinn tried taking Reaper's head off with his sword.

The blade got stuck halfway through, the flesh somehow trying to heal around it, but Quinn snarled, gripped it with both hands, and hacked away like he was chopping down a tree. Reaper's gun went off again, but the shot went wide. A few hacks later and Reaper's head detached and rolled across the platform.

Quinn huffed a triumphant cry and slumped against the wall.

Caius stepped onto the platform and stalked across it to where Reaper's head had stopped. When he nudged it over, Reaper's sneering face became visible, and Lukas was sure it was just a trick of the light when the eyes seemed to move.

Lukas glanced across the room to make sure Max and Akito were still standing and found they'd managed to subdue the mage with a cage of fire. He doubted they could hold it for long and hoped that with Reaper dead, whatever mages he had bound to him would be freed. He stepped over Reaper's corpse to get to Quinn, reaching for his elbow so he could check his shoulder, but the wound was already healing. It looked like the bullet had barely grazed him.

"That was a stupid risk," he muttered, smirking faintly when Quinn narrowed his eyes. "But also kinda hot. You should look into becoming a lumberjack."

Quinn reached up with his free hand to tangle his fingers in Lukas' hair before dragging him closer. He pressed their lips together despite the entire front of his body being splattered with blood. "I'll jack your lumber any day," he growled.

Lukas laughed while he tried to decide if he wanted to groan or cry more. "You've been spending far too much time with Max." He closed the distance to indulge in a kiss as the adrenaline faded, only to jerk away when Caius swore and fired his last few bullets.

He turned to see Reaper's head with several new wounds leaking liquidized aconite. Except, impossibly, they were slowly healing.

Quinn pushed past Lukas as he moved closer to the platform. "What in the Deadpool fuckery is going on!"

Across the room, the fire cage vanished with a soft whoosh, the temperature in the room immediately stabilizing as Max dropped to the floor with a tired laugh. "Finally."

"Nice job," Akito said, still standing over the storm mage, though they showed no sign of wanting to continue the fight anymore.

When Lukas turned back to Reaper, it was to see his blood spreading across the platform, unerringly heading straight for his body. "How is that even possible?" Sure, shifters had supernaturally fast healing, but beheading one was usually more than enough to kill them. No one moved as the blood continued spreading, and he was almost relieved when Reaper's head didn't speak.

Caius crouched next to the head, studying it for a moment before grabbing it by the hair. "Find a container to put this in," he said as he stood. A couple of the Wyoming pack slipped away.

Lukas would have suggested they burn Reaper to ashes, but judging by his face, someone had already tried that. When he glanced at Quinn, he saw his shoulder was fully healed with none of the scarring that should have been left behind by the aconite. Dread and disbelief tightened his gut. With the number of mages trapped downstairs….

He turned to Caius with a grimace. "There's something you need to see."

CHAPTER 24

TOUA ACCEPTED Leon's help with lighting and holding the incense. He knew he once again couldn't heal all of Rían's injuries completely, but he could at least fix the internal burns and fractured cheekbone. There was a familiar heavy weight pressing down on his magic, likely from the suppressors the Order liked to use in their so-called training, but since they weren't attuned to his magic signature, he could still function. It would just take a bit more effort and focus.

He carefully pressed his fingertips against Rían's face and closed his eyes as he shook the finger bells on his other hand. His dragon spirit answered immediately, coiling himself around Rían's head and shoulders, lighting up with a bright silver glow that was nearly blinding even though Toua wasn't looking at him directly. He kept a steady rhythm with the bells and focused on healing the worst of the damage.

He wanted to take away every bit of Rían's pain and erase the proof of the last twelve days, but even if he hadn't been worried sick the entire time and was fully rested that would be impossible; he still had to call Rían's spirit back to his body, and that could potentially take a lot out of him.

As the fractures and worst of the internal damage finished healing, he slowed the rhythm of the finger bells and pulled his hand away from Rían's face. He swayed sideways, and Leon caught him with a hand on his shoulder.

"All right?"

Toua managed a weak smile. "Fine." Leon didn't look convinced, but Toua didn't have the energy to persuade him. He tensed when the door at the top of the stairs opened, turning to make sure Reaper wasn't coming to try to get his hands on Rían again, but it was only Lukas with the rest of the pack in tow. With a soft breath of relief, Toua slumped forward to rest his head against Rían's knee.

He told himself they wouldn't be coming down here if Reaper hadn't been taken care of. When the footsteps stopped outside the cage, he lifted his head.

"How is he?" Lukas asked.

"Still needs a lot of healing." Toua glanced past Lukas, at the mages stirring in the cages, and was sure a lot of them would need healing too, but he wouldn't be able to focus on them until Rían was whole again.

"We should get him out of this cage," Quinn said.

"No!" Toua put his arms across Rían's legs as if that would be enough to stop them when he doubted he could even lift his bag right then. "I need to *ua neeb*." At their confused looks he made an impatient gesture. "I need to go into the spirit realm."

"Is he dead?" Quinn asked in alarm.

Toua scowled. "No." He didn't have time to explain. He wasn't sure how long Rían had been in this condition, but even a few hours was too long. The only silver lining was that this was likely where Rían had been the entire time, so Toua should have an easier time of guiding his spirit back.

"You already look exhausted," Lukas said quietly. "Can you handle that right now?"

Toua met his gaze and blew out a calming breath. He was tired, but he knew he wouldn't get any rest until Rían was back in one piece. It'd been a few years since he'd connected fully with the spirit realm, and he'd never strayed close to it as much as he had the past months. That alone was taking its own toll on him, but he could do this much. He had to. "I can do it," he said firmly.

Lukas frowned and glanced from him to Rían, who hadn't moved since they'd found him. His eyes were cracked open and he was breathing, but with his spirit wandering, his body was unresponsive. He may as well have been in a coma.

Toua didn't realize he expected to have to fight until Lukas nodded. "If you're sure. What do you need?"

He let out a shaky breath and reached for his bag. He really could have used his traditional clothing, but he hadn't exactly expected to have to cross into the spirit realm, and he'd been more concerned with replacing his tools. He was lucky enough to have retrieved his hood since it couldn't be easily replaced, and he hoped it would be enough. "Time."

"How long?" Quinn asked.

"I don't know. His spirit should know we're looking for him." He hoped it wouldn't take long, but if Rían's spirit knew where his body was and hadn't come back on its own or responded to Toua's healing…. Considering what Reaper had been doing to him, Toua wouldn't be surprised if he had a fight on his hands. "Reaper is dead?" he asked as he pulled out a candle, a white ribbon, and his hood. The container with a bit of rice and one of the cooked chickens he set aside to be left behind after he saved Rían.

When no one answered, Toua looked over, pausing on Quinn long enough to notice the blood covering him and deciding he didn't need to know how it got there. "Is he dead?" he demanded.

"Mostly," Lukas replied slowly.

"What the fuck does that mean?"

"It means we're working on it. He'll be fully dead soon," Quinn said.

Toua eyed him before looking at Caius. He was studying the cages with a frown, but he turned his attention to Toua when he noticed him watching.

"Reaper won't be harming anyone else," Caius said firmly. "Focus on saving Rían."

As much as Toua wanted answers, Rían was more important. He pulled out his finger bells and slipped the one with the black ribbon onto his thumb. Then he looped the white ribbon around Rían's wrist next to the frayed red one.

He wrapped the other end around his own wrist, then glanced at the incense before handing a fresh stick to Leon. He lit the candle and set it a safe distance away before handing over the lighter as well. "Do not let that burn out." Then he settled his hood back into place, set his txiab neeb beside him, the discs rattling loud in the close confines of the cell, picked up his sword with his free hand, and closed his eyes as he chanted under his breath.

No matter how many times he did it, slipping into the spirit realm was a bit disconcerting. Everything always looked the same, until he moved.

When he stood, the iron cage smeared away and left him standing outside. Only not in the desert. Rolling green hills spread out around him, a small village in one direction and sheer cliffs with giant waves crashing against them in the other. His surroundings blurred as he stepped to the edge of the village. He turned at the sound of children laughing and found a young Rían, maybe six or seven years old, making animal shapes out of several large bubbles floating in the air.

Younger kids were jumping around him, arms outstretched as they smacked the bubbles back and forth, the shapes changing after every hit. A cat turned into a fox. A dog into a cow.

The sky darkened, and the laughter screeched to an eerie halt.

Rían turned and spotted Toua, a blinding smile on his face, before he vanished into wisps of pale smoke.

Shadows stretched around Toua as the wind picked up, and he tightened his grip on his sword.

Lightning struck next to him and materialized into a young man with long black hair and mercury-silver eyes. He crossed his arms and glanced around with a bored expression. "You've caught something's attention."

Toua bit his tongue against telling the dragon how astute he was. "Are you going to take care of it?"

The dragon let out a pained sigh. "If I must."

"I'll make an offering of nqaj qaab zib when this is over," Toua promised; he wasn't above exploiting the dragon's fondness for his family's pork belly recipe. He caught the brief smile and nod of acceptance as he turned and stepped into the Order's library.

Rían was leaning over a pile of books spread across a table, flipping through pages with a familiar scowl. He'd always looked serious when he started his solo missions, like he was one wrong word from cursing someone with boils.

After their first meeting here, when Toua had given Rían his protective bracelet, the reference section of the library had become their secret. Rían escaped there whenever he had time to devour as much magical knowledge as he could. Toua went simply to enjoy Rían's presence. Even then Toua had been drawn to him, though it wasn't until he found Rían again and lost him that he understood the depth of that connection.

Toua stepped closer when he saw himself appear and lean over the table next to Rían. For a moment he thought it was merely a shadow of memory, but the flicker of gray-green skin, long ears, and sharp teeth proved otherwise. He lifted his sword and hurled it across the room, but the creature vanished with a screech before the blade could sink into its chest. It sailed through the afterimage and lodged in the bookshelf instead.

He retrieved his sword by leaping onto the table and walking across without looking away from it. Only when it was in his possession again did he turn to find Rían watching him with suspicious eyes. He held out his other hand, his finger bells jingling in the silence. "Come with me."

"Why?" Rían asked, leaning back and eyeing Toua's hand like it was a snake poised to strike.

"You need to come home."

Rían scoffed and took a step back. "I don't have a home," he said, then vanished.

Toua cursed and spun around, gasping as biting cold wind cut through him before he sank into calf-deep snow. "Fuck," he hissed, his hands already stinging. He couldn't see anything with the horizontal snow blowing into his face. "Rían," he whispered, flexing his wrist and blowing out a long breath as he focused on the ribbon binding them in the physical world.

He turned at the sound of low growls and felt more than saw the landscape shift around him again. When Rían came into view, he was holding off half a dozen large monsters. At least eight feet tall, they stood on two legs but looked more like wolves than humans. Ears, tails, dark fur, sharp teeth in snarling faces, and red eyes that glowed in the fading light.

Behind Rían were two children huddled together.

Bright spellworks swirled around them as Rían fought the wolfmen off. His bag was spilled open at his feet, jars half buried in the snow, but that didn't stop Rían from using them. Countless colors lit up the area like a mini aurora, a delicate weave and dance as Rían called on specific components at his feet, twisted them into spells, and set them loose.

A curtain of blue fire covered one of the wolfmen before a pink mist exploded in front of another. A burst like green fireworks forced one to take a few steps back, where a large glob of green glued it against another. Rían's amulets flared and sparked with power as one got close enough to knock him off his feet. Blood sprayed against the pure white snow, and Toua's chest tightened.

"Rían!" he shouted, running forward, but he wasn't needed.

Behind the wolfmen, a lance of condensed snow and ice lifted from the ground and sliced through the air, the edge sharp enough it severed each one through its torso. Rían cursed as he pushed to his feet and turned to the children behind him. "Go home," he ordered, waiting for them to scamper off before reaching for his bag with a wince.

Toua crouched next to him and held his hand out, but Rían scowled at him. "The feck you want?"

"You to stop being an idiot," Toua snapped. "Now take my hand so we can go home."

Instead of responding, Rían vanished. Again.

Toua slammed his fist into the snow where Rían had been sitting. "Fucking dammit, Rían! Stop running!" He rocked forward with a wordless yell before spinning to his feet. Next time he wasn't asking. He'd drag Rían's fucking soul back to his body kicking and screaming if he had to.

When he stepped forward the snow melted beneath an inferno.

Toua dropped to his knees to escape the heat as walls of smoke and flame billowed on every side of him. He crawled forward and came face-to-face with a dead body, his heart lurching before he could comprehend that it wasn't Rían. He coughed as smoke slipped beneath his hood and continued moving.

An ominous cracking slowly grew louder until the far wall ripped away from the house, the flames swirling higher as fresh oxygen poured in. And there, beneath a pile of debris, was Rían. The giant splinter of wood lodged in his leg told him where and when this memory belonged, and he wasn't surprised that it linked to Reaper.

He pushed the debris off Rían and dragged him to the edge where the wall had fallen away, then nearly lost his balance with vertigo when he made the mistake of looking out at the forest and very long drop below them. Removing the chunk of wood and healing Rían's leg was easy enough since he'd already done it in the physical realm.

Then he shook Rían until he jerked awake, and grasped his wrist so he couldn't get away again. He leaned in close when Rían focused on him. "I might be a healer, but I really want to strangle you right now."

Rían blinked at him. "Toua?" he asked, his voice rough from the smoke. "Not gonna lie, that'd be kinda hot."

Toua's body flushed hotter than the flames around them, and he was grateful for the hood shielding most of his face, but now was certainly not the time or the place. "Let's go. I need to get you back in your body." He kept hold of Rían as he pushed to his feet, but Rían didn't budge. Stifling his frustration, he squeezed Rían's wrist and tugged. "*Please*, let's go."

"I don't want to."

Toua sank to his knees again, carefully setting his sword between them so he had both hands free to wrap around Rían's. "They took care of Reaper," he said firmly, threading their fingers together when Rían visibly shuddered. "He'll never touch you or anyone else again."

Rían let out a shaky breath, staring at the flames as they continued to blaze around them without getting closer.

He wasn't sure how much time had passed in the physical world, but they couldn't linger. Especially with something hunting them. "You do have a home," he tried, squeezing Rían's hand. "Even if you don't want to join the pack, I'd… like to stay with you."

Rían's fingers twitched against Toua's, and he tilted his head towards him. "You can't really mean that," he whispered.

"Why not?"

"The only thing anyone ever wants me for is my magical talents."

Toua lifted his hand to flick the center of Rían's forehead, which earned him a familiar scowl as Rían finally looked at him.

"The feck was that for?"

"Yes, you might be a genius of a mage, but you're also brilliant, kind, and a patient teacher." He hadn't missed the way the younger kids would flock to Rían in the Order to ask questions, or beg him to teach them something new, or tell them about his latest mission. "And you're cute," he added, flicking Rían's forehead again when he rolled his eyes. "Now can we please go home?"

Rían tipped his head back with a profound sigh. "Fine."

Toua shook his head and picked up his sword as he stood again. This time Rían stood with him, and the burning room vanished beneath endless snow. As he turned to guide them back to their bodies, he had to wonder how he'd ended up with two drama kings in his life, only for the other said drama king to appear in front of them in a crackle of lightning.

He tightened his grips on Rían and his sword when he saw the blood and deep gash on the dragon's arm. "Not taking care of it, then?" he asked, hoping for an annoyed glare but getting a frustrated snarl instead. "What the fuck is it?"

"Fae," the dragon spat. "Or what's left of one."

Rían made a sound of surprise as the creature materialized in front of them, no longer hidden behind someone else's face. It wore a tattered black cloak and ripped pants, blood and bruises covering its exposed flesh. Its fingers ended in claws as sharp as its teeth.

"*Do not* let go," Toua hissed, gripping Rían's hand tighter with a jingle of his finger bells. His sword vanished in favor of his txiab neeb, the metal a solid weight in his hand. When he swiped it through the air across his body the clamor of the discs was far louder than in the physical realm. It also pulsed with magic as white energy sliced through the air, but instead of driving the creature away, it only seemed to piss it off.

The creature screamed, the high pitch threatening to deafen him, until a transparent wall appeared in front of them and blocked the sound.

Toua blinked and glanced at the dragon, who looked as confused as Toua. He turned to Rían and found him with his bag restored and a small jar of starlight in his free hand.

Rían shrugged and switched the jar for another that had a separator between two liquids.

The dragon turned and stared at it with a slow smirk before snatching it from Rían. "Run," he said, ignoring Rían's protest as he rushed forward.

Toua didn't hesitate to make a break for it, reaching for the touch of the ribbon binding him to Rían in the physical world to guide them back.

An explosion from behind them shook the earth and cracked the deep snow around them, and then they were falling into a bottomless crevice that split open beneath them.

Rían cursed and threw a jar with a spell word that broke the glass and formed a swirling vortex. Instead of sucking them in, it pushed them higher, throwing them out of the chasm. They hit the snow and rolled, coming to a stop against the hard legs of a table and chairs in a painful tangle of limbs.

Toua pushed himself up with a groan, sure his arm would have broken if they'd been in the physical world. "Okay?" he asked as they helped each other to their feet.

"Been better."

"Almost there," Toua said, reaching for the white thread again and pulling them towards it. The library melted away into the green hills of Rían's childhood home, but as soon as the grass solidified beneath them, the sky darkened and crackled with lightning, and not the friendly lightning of his dragon spirit. Thunder cracked through the sky with enough force to shatter the windows of the nearby village.

"Fuck," Toua snarled. He could feel the ribbon beneath his fingers, the physical realm *right there*, but as he turned to guide them back to the cell with their bodies, the creature appeared in front of them, dozens of sharp blood-stained teeth on display as it screamed. The fact it was missing an arm was no consolation when its remaining hand aimed for his heart, its claws curled as if it meant to rip him open.

Rían jerked him back in time for only his shirt to tear.

He slashed with his sword. The blade sliced across the fae's arm, but it didn't seem to do anything except piss it off further.

"Do you have iron?"

"*Why* would I have iron?" he asked, defensively striking to keep the creature from getting any closer.

Rían cursed and ripped his hand out of Toua's grip.

"Rían!" he yelled, fighting the instinct to turn and grab hold of him again. The fae screeched and tried to follow Rían, but Toua threw himself into its path. "You're not getting him," he snarled, forcing the fae back. Standing between it and Rían seemed like a great idea until the fae turned its full focus on Toua. The eerie blue glow of its eyes hit him with a near-paralyzing fear and the instinct to run, but he knew he couldn't. They were too close to returning to their bodies to risk getting separated and lost in the spirit realm here.

The creature came at him with all the fury of a tormented spirit.

Toua wasn't the strongest of fighters, but he could hold his own. Hopefully long enough for Rían to do whatever he was planning. He took more hits than he dealt as he blocked or sidestepped everything he could. He had no intention of moving to the offensive, he doubted he'd ever be able to kill it, but every step he was pushed back put the fae that much closer to Rían.

It wasn't until the fae lunged at him and his back hit a wall that he realized how far he'd moved. Toua raised his sword and slashed at the hand about to rip him apart, which left him hard-pressed to protect his throat from sharp teeth. He jabbed his free hand into the fae's neck, but that didn't slow it down. Hot putrid breath wafted under his hood as it closed in on him.

"Hey, fangface!" Rían shouted.

The fae ripped away from Toua and turned towards Rían, who was waiting to jam an iron fire poker through its skull. Its mouth opened with a horrendous screech before it vanished in a burst of blood and mist.

"Told you," Toua panted, shoving off the side of the house and grabbing Rían's hand. "Brilliant." He reached for the thread between them and pulled them into the cage. Rían balked when he realized where they were, but Toua squeezed his fingers tighter. "It's all right," he said softly. "He's gone. And I healed the worst of your injuries. I'll heal the rest soon."

Rían stared at him a long moment before giving a jerky nod.

He squeezed Rían's fingers one last time before guiding his spirit back where it belonged. He chanted softly under his breath to complete the ritual before thanking the spirits, then turned and stepped back into his own body.

CHAPTER 25

RÍAN REALLY did not like pain.

He groaned as he woke up to an aching body and no memory of why it hurt. A strange sound escaped his parched throat as panic slammed into him. Whatever had happened, his body remembered it vividly.

"It's okay, it's okay."

He blinked as Toua's face appeared in front of him. "No," he rasped. Toua couldn't be here. Toua was supposed to be safe far, far away from here.

"It's okay," Toua said again. "Reaper is… mostly dead. But you're safe, I promise."

Rían's breath hitched with disbelief. That couldn't be true. This was *not real, not real, not real*. But he could taste the iron of the cage around him and feel the mild burn in his nose from being forced so close to it. He slumped forward with a sob and let Toua take his weight. He couldn't really believe Reaper was dead until he saw proof for himself, but if Toua was here, the pack had to be here, and he trusted Caius to at least protect his pack.

Time went wonky for a bit.

He remembered climbing stairs and sitting on a comfortable couch as voices spoke nonsense around him. A hot drink in his hands, the lingering taste of a boiled egg, and a blanket wrapped around him. The light was a different angle whenever he thought to pay attention to it, and he knew hours were passing, but every time he looked beside him to make sure he wasn't dreaming, either Toua or Lukas was right there.

"You should take him home," Caius said, which was the first thing he'd understood since Toua pulled him out of the cage.

"No," Rían said, swallowing against the grainy feeling in his throat. He couldn't leave, though he couldn't remember exactly why. Not until he took in the rest of the room for the first time and saw the storm mage tucked into the corner of the other couch. "The mages." He leaned forward, spilling lukewarm tea over his fingers before Lukas took it away. "They need help." He blinked as Caius sat on the coffee table in front of him.

"We're helping them," Caius said firmly. "And we'll need your help too, but you're no use to anyone while you're in shock." Rían opened his mouth to protest, but Caius narrowed his eyes. "Toua is no use either, when he's running on fumes," he said, pitching his voice louder as he glanced towards the kitchen.

"I'm fine."

"Both of you, go home," Caius ordered. "Shower, eat, rest. Come back in two days."

Rían scowled, but he didn't have the strength to argue. He did have the strength to ask, "What did you mean, mostly dead?"

Caius' calm expression twitched before he let out a sharp breath. "Reaper seems to have the ability to survive being decapitated. Among other things."

Rían stared, then turned his head to stare at Lukas, waiting for him to make it make sense.

"We have a theory it's because he has so many mages bound to him," Lukas replied with a helpless shrug. "Max is working on breaking the bindings with Akito, but it's slow going. As soon as he's really dead, we'll let you know."

"Until then, go home. Can you get back yourself, or do you need Akito?" Caius asked.

Rían nearly scoffed, but he knew the dangers of opening a doorway when not completely aware of one's surroundings. "Get Aki," he grumbled.

Caius nodded and stood, and Lukas bumped an elbow against his arm. "Glad to have you back, squirrel." Then he stood and let Toua take his place.

Toua gave him a tired smile and squeezed his hand.

Akito stepped into the room a moment later, complaining about not being anyone's chauffeur, but he studied Rían with a critical eye and a faint nod. "Glad you're not dead," he said as he opened a doorway. "And please make sure the idiots we left behind have eaten something," he added before ushering them through and promptly closing the doorway.

Toua snorted softly and tugged Rían upstairs to Toua's room, and the moment Rían saw the sugar glider cage, he sank to his knees with a broken sob. Toua landed on the floor next to him. "What's wrong?"

"Niamh," he rasped, but that was all he managed to get out. Even as he reached for the familiar bond, the guilt and anguish he felt over losing her evaporated into relief. A soft squeak from the cage announced her presence as she scurried out of one of the hanging tents and sailed across the room. "You're okay," he whispered, a choked laugh escaping him as both her siblings joined her in tucking themselves against his neck.

"They found her," Toua said, rubbing a finger against the albino's head. "We wondered where they'd gone off to," he added when Rían gave him a bleary, confused look. "Come on, get some sleep."

Rían sank onto the edge of the bed and tightened his hold on Toua's hand when he started to pull away. "Stay?"

"Of course. Just give a minute to make sure Caleb and Dante have eaten something."

Rían nodded and forced his fingers to loosen; then he sat on the bed and focused on breathing and the soft furry warmth of his sugar gliders for endless minutes until Toua returned. It wasn't until they were all settled under the covers and Toua draped an arm over him that Rían relaxed enough to let himself sleep. He found Toua's hand and curled his fingers around it, counting his heartbeats to the steady rhythm of *real, real, real*.

Reaper was as good as dead. Toua was safe. Max and Akito were safe. Their familiars were safe.

Rían was safe.

IT TOOK days before that knowledge started to sink in, and even then Rían still had moments of irrational fear and panic. He kept losing bits of time too, though Toua, Max, and Lukas all worked to bring him back before he'd been gone too long.

Toua healed his body, but it didn't stop the phantom aches or pains. Or the nightmares that had him waking in the middle of the night, gasping for air. Only the fact that Toua was always there when it happened kept him from losing his mind on top of losing sleep.

Sorting through the mages Reaper had abducted was a slow and tedious process, but at least breaking their bindings seemed to slowly weaken Reaper's healing ability. Max was breaking the bindings of the remaining mages in the basement the second day Rían stepped back inside the house, which was the only reason he could believe it when Reaper was finally truly dead. The recoil as the balance tipped, the magic no longer able to sustain Reaper, was powerful enough to cause a faint tremor of an earthquake that rattled the windows and dishes in the cupboards. The rest of the bindings snapped the moment the bastard's head stopped trying to reattach itself to his body.

Once that was done, they all breathed a bit easier and could focus on the task of freeing the mages. Some of them, like Aliyah, hadn't been there long enough to go mad or completely shut down, but all of them were severely traumatized. Rían spent most of his time and energy making shielding rings for each one who had family or someone they trusted to return to. And then there were a few like Amelia, who'd spoken out against the Order and vanished.

Akito had found a second, smaller basement on the other side of the house, where a few pregnant women were being kept. From their stories, high-rank mages in the Order would come by every few months, choose a woman, and Reaper would use his bindings to make her complicit. Once the children were old enough to walk and talk, the Order would whisk them away, bypassing the world laws in every way possible.

"We can't let them keep doing this shit," Lukas snapped, pacing the edge of the large room.

"We won't," Caius said, and something in the way he said it made Rían blink and focus on him. "Quinn mentioned you have a way to keep the Order out of our territory."

Rían's stomach flip-flopped, sure this was a dream. Except none of his dreams were pleasant anymore. "Yeah," he whispered before clearing his throat. "I haven't tested them, but I found the old bylaw spells. They're simple to cast, but the territory has to be covered by the mage casting the spell. Or mages," he said with a glance at Toua.

"Covered by walking?" Caius asked.

Rían shrugged. "It's not specific. It's more that the territory needs to be marked out by the magic. I assume driving would accomplish that."

"That's a lot of ground to cover," Lukas murmured. "Can it be done in sections?"

"Maybe, but you run the risk of missing an area and leaving a spot unprotected."

"We could try with the house first," Max suggested.

"Not this one," Akito said. "We're already on borrowed time before the Order shows up here. If it doesn't work, it'll only tip our hand."

"Packhouse, then," Caius said. "If it works, we'll do the same to the city. Then we can start moving the mages there and get them the help they need."

Rían took a shaky breath and glanced down when Toua squeezed his hand. Despite Reaper being dead, the Order was always the bigger threat, and only when they were incapable of coming near them would Rían ever have a chance of truly feeling safe again.

CHAPTER 26

TOUA FINISHED putting his supplies away on his altar and set out the small cups with a bit of water, rice, and nqaj qaab zib as offerings. He'd lost contact with his dragon spirit for a few days. Apparently the fae creature had done a number on him before coming after Toua and Rían, but he'd finally sensed the dragon again yesterday and had spent all night cooking to keep his promise.

He pressed several sticks of incense into the large bowls of uncooked rice at the top, then sat back to check everything was in place. He spent several minutes thanking his dragon for his help and asked for his continued assistance in the future.

Then he sat back and steeled himself to get back to work.

He'd healed what mages he could as the pack freed the ones who were coherent, but there was only so much he could do for years of trauma and imprisonment. Most of them would need years of professional care, which they couldn't get until the city was guaranteed safe from Order interference.

Toua stood from the altar and headed downstairs, where Quinn and Lukas were working on the plan for if the bylaw spells worked. One of the monitors had a map of the city, with the roads they'd be using highlighted in four different colors. Instead of the boundary of the city itself, they'd take the highway toll connections that formed a misshapen circle around the majority of the city and smaller towns around it. One of them would jump on 121 to avoid the sharp arrow into their territory. There was no easy way to secure the airport, but at least the main road out of it would be inside the barrier.

From the looks of the map, it meant at least half an hour of casting for each of them, but if they did it in the middle of the night, maybe they'd escape traffic.

Lukas straightened from where he was leaning over Quinn's shoulder to glance at Toua. "You all ready for the test?"

Toua nodded despite the nerves twisting his stomach. Rían hadn't lied when he said the spell was simple, but even warding their house against the Order seemed like a declaration of war. He couldn't imagine how the Order would react if they took a city.

Lukas squeezed Toua's shoulder. "It'll be fine."

"Considering the past few weeks, I don't think your definition of fine is to be trusted," he said tightly.

Lukas dropped his hand and stepped back, sitting on the edge of the L-shaped desk instead.

Quinn swiveled his chair around. "What's wrong?"

He bit his tongue against saying *everything*. There wasn't anything truly wrong; in fact, things were about as good as could be expected right then. Maybe he was reeling from how his problems had been solved. He didn't have the cartel after him anymore. Reaper was dead. Caleb and Dante were safe too, even if they were prone to keeping in their room for now. Other than all the mages, Rían included, that Reaper had tormented, everything else was… fine.

"Nothing," Toua finally murmured.

Quinn raised a dubious eyebrow, but Toua pretended not to see it.

Lukas cleared his throat. "How's Rían doing?"

"Better," Toua answered. Rían still had moments when he spaced out, but Toua had put together a soul-locking bracelet for him to make sure his spirit didn't wander off again. He'd made a proper protection charm with blue, red, and white strings too, though Rían still refused to take off the simple red ribbon.

An awkward silence fell between them, and Toua realized he didn't have any real reason to be bothering them, but Caius and Max saved him from having to make some excuse to leave.

Caius handed over a paper to Quinn while Max stepped into Lukas' personal space and leaned against Quinn's shoulder. "It's good, right?" Max said.

"We're publicly claiming the city?" Quinn asked.

"Apparently we'll have to for the spells to hold," Caius said, though he didn't sound happy about it. "This needs to break on the morning news after the spells are set, if the spells work on the house. I'll meet with the mayor before we do the city."

Toua leaned over to read the paper, his eyebrows creeping higher as he read. Once the bylaw spells were activated, any mage or person bound to or working for the Order would have twenty-four hours to leave the city before the spells would forcibly evict them.

There were also instructions for those with bindings to call a number if they wanted the bindings removed. "Smart," he murmured. There were enough stores selling magical supplies in the city that most of them were likely run by low-level mages who the Order still kept tabs on.

Once the city was free of the Order, they'd be able to move the rest of the imprisoned mages in to get the care they needed to recover. "Have you found a decent care facility yet?" Toua asked.

"I bought one yesterday," Caius said.

Toua stared at him before glancing at Max, who was smirking and patting Caius' chest. "My father had apparently been in negotiations for one to lock me up in. Caius took over on the condition it be a facility focused on helping mages abandoned by the Order."

"Don't worry, I'm running thorough background checks on all the staff," Quinn said. "No one will be working there if the Order even so much as breathes near them."

That was reassuring, at least. He could only hope all this preparation wasn't in vain.

CHAPTER 27

RÍAN STOOD at one corner of the packhouse property and glanced towards Max and Toua standing at the adjacent corners. Only when they glanced at Akito on the opposite side and gave him a nod did they start the spell.

They'd decided to do the full property line rather than only the house, which meant he didn't need to adjust the fences to give them a clear path. As one, they started moving clockwise around the perimeter. The magic swirled around them as soon as they took their first step, growing in strength with every step after. It built with the force of a storm around Rían, as if he were in the eye of a tornado, and for a moment he wondered if the spell was some kind of trap. But he'd studied the spells for months. He was certain this one was meant to claim territory as their own and declare it off-limits to the Order.

Except when he reached the corner Max had started at, the magic was still building. Max was at the far corner, and when he glanced back, Toua was at the one Rían had left. So he kept walking, his heart hammering. If the spell didn't latch and set, this much power buildup was going to rip something to pieces, most likely starting with the mages casting it.

A few steps later, he felt the shift. The magic transferred to the path they'd walked, lighting up the perimeter in a brilliant gold shield that was visible to the naked eye. A perfect ward that extended far into the air and deep into the earth.

Max whooped and pumped a fist into the air, and Rían could hear Akito crowing on the other side. When he turned to Toua, he was already halfway to Rían, and he moved to meet him.

He didn't question how natural it felt to wrap his arms around Toua's waist, to pull him in close, or to press a kiss to his lips.

Toua squeaked in surprise before throwing his arms around Rían's neck and kissing him back.

Max wolf-whistled, and Rían freed a hand enough to flip him off before pulling Toua inside and up to their room.

Borrowed room. They'd need to move into one of the spares soon, and he'd have to decide if he was willing to officially join the pack, but those were both problems to worry about later.

When they reached the bedroom and Rían closed the door, Toua tensed. "I uh… I should have told you before now that I'm not… I mean, I like you, and that kiss was nice, but I don't…."

Rían closed the distance between them and squeezed Toua's hand. "You're not interested in sex."

Toua blinked at him, his mouth hanging open in surprise. "How?"

Rían shrugged. "Your aura," he said, pressing a finger to Toua's forehead before trailing his fingertip down Toua's nose, across his cheek and jaw and throat, to his heart, and back and forth across his chest, before stopping at his hip near his groin. "Your sexual desire line is mostly gray."

"My what?" Toua asked, his aura sparkling with confusion, relief, and baffled amusement.

Rían dropped onto the edge of the bed, his body almost shaking with his own relief. He hadn't realized how tense he'd been, waiting for the Order to retaliate or send someone else after him, until that tension was gone. "Your sexual desire line."

Toua sat next to him and blew out a breath. "That doesn't bother you?"

"No. I can also see how loyal you are and that for some reason you're completely obsessed with me."

Toua elbowed him with a soft snort. "Obsessed is a strong word."

"Infatuated?" Rían smirked when Toua narrowed his eyes. "Besotted?"

"Annoyed sounds more accurate," Toua muttered even as he leaned closer.

Rían failed to stifle a laugh. "Liar," he whispered against Toua's lips.

"Shut up and kiss me."

"If I have to." Rían twitched back with a startled laugh when Toua pinched his side, then suddenly found himself on his back with Toua straddling his hips.

Toua's eyes were wide, and shock sparked through his aura, as surprised by his own actions as Rían was.

"If you wanted to be on top that badly you could have just asked."

Toua planted his hands on either side of Rían's head and narrowed his eyes. "I'm starting to see why people call you insufferable."

"Rude. I'm perfectly sufferable." He would have said more, but Toua closed the distance between them, and Rían lost himself in the feel and taste of Toua's lips. He hooked his arms around Toua, pulling him closer before rolling them farther onto the bed. He'd rarely made out with someone for the sake of making out, but kissing Toua was grounding. He couldn't get lost in his own head when the heat of Toua's body was pressed into him.

Toua smelled like the spices he'd used for lunch and the green tea soap he'd taken a liking to thanks to Akito. Even if Rían knew it wouldn't lead to anything, he was still worked up by the time they broke apart to catch their breaths.

Toua pressed his thigh higher where it was trapped between Rían's legs. "Do you need to take care of that?"

Rían squeezed his eyes shut as he swallowed a groan and fought the urge to rock into Toua. "Not right now."

"You could… if you wanted to."

He cracked his eyes open to study Toua. "You want me to jerk off in front of you?"

"Not *right* in front of me." Toua flushed and pulled back a bit before waving a hand between them. "You could get under the covers or something."

Rían shook his head with a soft laugh, but he wiggled around until he could get the covers over himself. Never had he imagined he'd finally end up in bed with Toua, sleeping beside him at night as if that was where he belonged, only to get himself off under the covers after making out. Once he was comfortable, he glanced at Toua. "You're sure?"

Toua pressed against him again and slid a hand into Rían's hair. "You look good when you're enjoying yourself," he murmured, nudging Rían onto his back before kissing him again.

Rían sank into the pleasure building up again, his fingers lingering at the top of his jeans. It was too weird being the only one to get off, but when Toua nuzzled across Rían's cheek to his ear and whispered, "Touch yourself," it was less weird and more exciting.

A strangled moan escaped him as he got his pants undone and wrapped his fingers around himself. He tilted his head as he sought out Toua's lips again and wasn't able to stifle a whimper from the slide of Toua's hot tongue against his. He kept his eyes cracked open, needing to see Toua to know this was real, despite it being far too pleasurable to be a dream.

Toua caught his eye and smiled, resting a hand on Rían's cheek and swiping his thumb where the deep gash had been. He pressed their foreheads together, his other hand flexing and massaging the back of Rían's head. "I'm here. You're safe," he whispered against Rían's lips.

He let out a shuddering gasp, working his free hand from under the covers to wrap around Toua and grip the back of his shirt. He wanted to draw this out, make it last as long as they'd been kissing before, but then Toua hiked a leg up enough to nudge between Rían's legs, panting against his cheek as if Toua was as turned on as he was.

Toua's whispered, "Let me see you come," was the hottest thing anyone had ever said to him, and his body responded in kind with the most intense orgasm he'd had in years.

Rían was sure he lost a bit of time after, but it wasn't the same as before. There was no sense of being trapped in a body that wasn't his or panic over when the pain would come again. If anything, he was more grounded than he'd been since leaving the Order, the world sharper, brighter, and far more brilliant than he ever thought it could be.

Toua nuzzled his cheek with a smile before pulling back. He rolled off the bed and snatched up the towel from his shower that morning.

Rían snorted as Toua tossed the towel at his face. Once he'd cleaned himself up and they settled against each other again, he could almost start to believe he'd be okay.

LUKAS SLIPPED out of his own bed when he heard someone in the kitchen in the middle of the night. He caught Rían's scent before he made it out of the hallway, then the sharp, tangy scent of what little sweet pork belly was leftover. It was the second batch Toua had made, and it disappeared only slightly slower than the first.

"Couldn't sleep?" he asked, pausing when he noticed the deeper scent clinging to Rían. Catching Toua's scent on him was a matter of course since they'd moved into the same room, but this was the first time either of them had smelled like sex. He waited a moment to see if that would bother him, but it didn't. He'd already decided he wasn't interested in a one-time thing with Rían, and after everything that happened, it was clear Toua and Rían shared a far deeper connection than Lukas had suspected in the beginning.

"Not really," Rían said, pushing the dish with half the leftovers closer once he'd filled his own plate.

Lukas found a fork and took the container to the table, eyeing Rían when he sat across from him. "Sorry we didn't get to you sooner," he said softly, hating the way Rían froze, his scent spiking with too many emotions to name, but all of them negative.

After a long moment he blew out a breath and his scent mostly cleared. "You found me," Rían said. "That's what matters."

Lukas nodded and took a bite. "So you and Toua finally got together," he said, smirking when Rían glowered at him. "Congrats."

"Sure you're not jealous?"

"Nope. I have to put up with you enough as it is. I don't need sex complicating that." He met and held Rían's gaze for a long moment to make sure Rían knew he was sincere. Then he got up to put the leftovers back in the fridge and patted Rían's shoulder on his way by. "Good talk."

CHAPTER 28

FOUR DAYS later, Rían sat in the passenger seat of a rental on the side of the highway, tapping his fingers in an impatient rhythm against his knee. Nerves left an unpleasant heat in his gut, and he silently cursed the rest of the pack for being so slow to get in position. It was after midnight. They should have been there by now.

"Jesus, you're starting to make even me nervous," Quinn said from the driver's seat.

Rían curled his fingers into a tight fist and slanted a quick look at Quinn from the corner of his eye. He wasn't exactly happy about being paired with Quinn, all things considered, and he might have believed this was some kind of revenge if not for the wolf's calm aura. Eager excitement and the desire to stick it to the Order were bright lines of orange, but there was no jealousy or anger that Rían could see.

"So," Quinn said, his too casual tone setting Rían even more on edge. "You and Toua are official now? No more pining and sappy staring, right?"

"Oh feck off. Like you have any room to talk," Rían muttered, turning his attention out the window, but he couldn't quite control the smile tugging at his lips. Their new bedroom furniture had arrived yesterday, a Victorian style in rich walnut wood, and they'd moved out of Max's room last night. Their relationship wasn't exactly a secret with five shifters and two nosy-as-fuck mages under the same roof, but the fact they hadn't taken a bedroom each somehow made it feel more real.

He ignored Quinn's snickering and was saved from any further conversation when Quinn's phone rang. It took a minute to get all four shifter-and-mage pairs on the line, but they all chimed in with a "Ready."

Rían started the chant, and Toua, Max, and Akito joined in. Once the magic started building, he motioned for Quinn to start driving. It didn't take long to realize the difference between casting this around their home and over an entire city. If he'd thought they were trapped in a tornado before, this was a category five hurricane.

Quinn swore as the force of magic threatened to drag them off the highway. Lukas' muffled curses said the others weren't faring much better, but Rían couldn't do anything to help. If he stopped casting or lost focus, it would disrupt the spell, and who knew what kind of backlash that could cause. Damaging the highways would be one of the best potential outcomes.

The tension growing in the others' voices was audible, but Toua and Akito were trained by the Order. They wouldn't break the spell unless they lost the ability to speak. Max was the weak link between them, but he'd apparently held up under pressure when the Order sent Akito after him in December. Rían could only hope he stayed focused for the next twenty-odd minutes.

The third time Quinn lost control, the grating of concrete against Rían's door made him falter. He grabbed the oh shit handle and closed his eyes, tuning out everything else and raising his voice to be heard over the deafening whine of raw power.

The weight of the gathering magic pressed down on him until he was sure he'd suffocate. Something warm and wet trickled from his nose, and he tasted blood at the back of his throat. There was a creak like something threatening to break and the snarling of shifters, but none of that could matter now.

This was likely the worst plan he'd ever come up with. Destroying an entire city if this blew up in their faces would certainly make it to the history books and solidify the Order's hold on the rest of the world in the aftermath.

Minutes dragged into hours. Surely they were past Max's starting point by now. He cracked his eyes open to see Quinn driving at an angle to stay on the road. Maybe he should have spared some time to put protections on the cars. Too late now. The amulets they all wore would have to be enough.

Like before, one moment the magic was a crushing weight, and the next it suddenly transferred from harnessed energy to completed spell. It snapped into place around and beneath them with the force of a small earthquake. The car jerked with a loud squealing of tires as the pressure Quinn was fighting against vanished. They spun twice before screeching to a halt, black tread marks squiggling out in front of them.

"Status," Caius demanded, and a weak chorus echoed back as everyone confirmed they were alive.

Rían swiped the back of his hand across his nose. It came away with a smear of blood, but a second pass showed nothing fresh.

Quinn whistled. "Looks like it really worked."

He glanced up to find the night sky lit up gold. A giant shimmering dome stretched out above them. Magic crackled and exploded like fireworks as the spell reached the net the Order placed over big cities to detect mages Sparking, completely destroying it. "Pretty sure they noticed that," he said dryly, swallowing the shaky laugh of disbelief bubbling in his throat.

Rían fumbled for his seat belt before climbing out of the car. He tipped his head back and watched as the net fizzled and died, removing the last bit of the Order's access to the city. When he breathed deep, he tasted ozone and freedom.

THE EARTHQUAKE hadn't been localized to the area of the casting. The entire city felt it, though thankfully there was no significant damage. It at least helped prove Caius' message was real when the news aired it that morning. The prerecorded interview laid out their pack's official claim over the territory and their reasoning for banning the Order. After the numerous attacks on Max that winter, followed by the Order's recent attempt to kill Rían, one of the most respected mages to work with the armed forces, Caius cast a vote of no confidence against the Order.

"We've already dealt with one corrupt crime lord in this city," Caius said, glancing from the interviewer to the camera. "We have no intention of disrupting the status quo further, so long as there are no more attacks against us. As for any mages in the city, if you need a binding broken, we can help. You have twenty-four hours before the barrier forcibly ejects you. If you're a parent of a young mage, we can help. You no longer need to worry about the Order taking your child."

Within days the public was a mix of those who wholeheartedly approved and those who vehemently did not. Thankfully, as the four of them were the only mages who claimed the city as their home through pack bonds, there wasn't much anyone could do about it.

Max had broken the bindings of at least six mages, including the owner of the shop he'd bought the outrageous amount of supplies from. They were even getting calls from mages in other parts of the state wanting theirs broken. Thankfully Caius wasn't stupid, and Rían hadn't even needed to argue for them to set up a securely warded area outside their territory boundary.

None of them thought the Order would be above setting a trap in retaliation. The Order had been suspiciously silent on the entire issue, refusing to even respond to the numerous news stations who called on them for a statement, but Rían was sure they knew Reaper had been disposed of by now. Which meant their little mage farm had been discovered.

The fact Caius had kept it all quiet for now was likely buying them some time, but sooner or later, someone would start questioning the facility that had opened almost overnight. Especially when it came to light that it was full of over fifty mages with severe PTSD and signs of abuse.

Rían would leave the politics to Caius and Max. He might have officially joined the pack, but he intended to focus on his shop and stocking up on his supplies for the fight that was sure to come.

They'd added the mage healer symbol to the shop window, right beside the eye with the line through it, at Toua's insistence that he help as much as he could. Which, at the moment, apparently meant sleeping on the couch while Rían worked through turning their plethora of base components into the powders and mixtures more commonly needed in spells. Not that Rían could blame him. Toua had done the first of at least six minor surgeries on Caius the evening before, which had depleted a lot of his energy. For now he was using his empty shop for the process, but he'd been promised his greenhouse and shed workshop would be delivered and set up by the end of the week. Then he'd be able to properly set to work on expanding their supply of potions and amulets.

Toua and Max might not appreciate the benefit of having a dozen amulets at their disposal, but Akito and Quinn had shown interest, and Rían was happy to oblige. Working his magic was grounding, and he welcomed the chance to apply his skills to a good cause for once.

He finished processing his share of the Satan's jellyfish and carefully split it between four jars for later, then sealed them and peeled his gloves off to call it a day. He hadn't had a single customer all afternoon, but he wouldn't complain about being bored anytime soon.

He stood and stretched his arms over his head, glancing out the window and pausing as two magpies settled in the shop window. They perched there and seemed to stare at him for a long moment before flying away. *One for sorrow, two for joy*, he thought as he walked over to the couch. He stopped to watch Toua sleep for a moment before leaning over the arm and kissing his nose, then his cheek when he didn't wake up. Then his lips. "Now I know you're faking," he said. When Toua still didn't respond, he pinched Toua's nose.

Toua smacked his hand away with a laugh. "Are you trying to suffocate me?"

"I'm hungry and want to go home." Which was a concept he wasn't sure he'd ever get used to. The last couple of years he'd known he'd be lucky to survive long enough to be free of the Order, much less fully escape their grasp. *Home* was one of the first things the Order took from their mages, but now, with the barrier firmly in place, it was only fitting he finally reclaim it for himself.

Toua rolled to his feet and pulled Rían closer with a slow smile. "Yeah. Let's go home."

See how the story started in
Mage's Marines
by Saria Bryant!

CHAPTER 1

MAX CRASHED to the floor, his vision swimming from the pistol cracking against his temple. The boot to his ribs was completely unnecessary; he was already caught. As he choked on air and the taste of blood, he forced himself upright. It wouldn't keep more punishment from raining down on him, but he'd be damned if he gave his father the satisfaction of seeing him writhe on the floor.

He swayed to the side, swallowing against the twisting of his stomach as the room spun out and away from him. He was intimately familiar with the signs of a potential concussion, but that was the least of his problems right now.

When he could finally focus, he recognized the dining room. Not the small one the family used. This was the big one, meant to impress and intimidate, which meant when he'd been dragged in here, he'd interrupted a business meeting.

A borderline hysterical laugh bubbled up in his chest, and he pressed his hand to his mouth to keep silent, focusing on the pain of his broken fingers to steady himself.

Blood trickled into his eye as he blinked at his father, who was staring at Max with familiar disappointment and loathing from the head of the table. He knew better than to look away, but he couldn't help it as his gaze slipped sideways, black and bright spots fighting for territory in his vision.

When he focused again, he was staring at a strange man sitting near his father, a bodyguard standing behind him. Handsome enough that even through the fog and muffled panic filling his mind, Max noticed the storm-cloud-gray eyes, strong, scruff-covered jaw, and black, silver-touched hair long enough to run his fingers through.

That was all the confirmation he needed. He was delirious.

The laughter tried to escape again, but when Jake stalked into the room from behind him and bowed to his father, Max's blood went cold.

"Your son, as promised," Jake said, his lips twisting into a sneer as he glanced at Max.

"No," Max whispered, refusing to believe it. But how else had they caught him so quickly? He'd planned for *months* to ensure he got away clean. He'd learned plenty of lessons from his previous attempts. Everything had been perfect. He just had to get to the airport and he could disappear into Asia, where his father had no power and no contacts.

Jake was the one person he trusted enough to tell his plans to, who had promised to drive Max's car as a decoy while Max took his motorcycle for the extra speed and maneuverability.

Max had even paid him a few thousand dollars for the trouble.

His father gestured to one of his men, and Jake turned, obviously expecting some reward. "Your services are appreciated. Your betrayal to my blood is not."

Jake realized too late his mistake. "Wait," he said, but that was all he got out. He wasn't nearly fast enough to dodge the bullet.

Max flinched from the sharp, muffled sound of the silenced gun, unable to look away as Jake's body slumped towards the floor, before it was dragged away by his father's men. He should have felt remorse or revulsion, but that was hardly the first corpse he'd seen, and even the sting of betrayal barely registered against the dozen stabbing and pulsing pains in his body.

His father sighed, an exaggerated sound Max knew was meant for him. "I warned you last time I would not tolerate this nonsense again, Max."

Nonsense. Like him wanting his own life, away from the violence and blood his father traded in, away from the suffocating control that took away his choices of when and what to eat, when to sleep, when to piss, was nonsense.

"I'm sorry, Father," he said, the words slipping out before he could stop them, much less control the thick sarcasm that came with them. "I really thought this would be the last time."

Fury and disgust twisted the man's face before he straightened. "You are no longer my son. I should have disowned you the moment I learned you were a *twink*."

Max couldn't help it. The hysterical laughter escaped. Never in his life did he ever think he would hear that word from the homophobic asshole's mouth. The man had made no secret of despising Max's *proclivities*. Not since the day Max made the mistake of telling his mother that he found a boy cute when he was five.

His life had been a waking nightmare ever since.

The punch to the back of his head to shut him up wasn't at all surprising. He nearly went to the floor again, but somehow stayed on his knees. "Dis'n me then," he slurred, spitting blood and hoping it stained the flawless wooden floor. "Or fuc'n kill me. I don't... care anymore." Death would be preferable to one more day in this hellhole.

He listed to the side as his vision wavered and went black.

CHAPTER 2

CAIUS WATCHED the young man slump to the floor with a mix of shock and dismay. Instincts shouted at him to get a medic as the scent of blood filled his nose, but common sense stayed his hand. He was no longer an acting colonel. Technically, he was a civilian now, and sitting in a mafia boss' home wasn't exactly the best place to reveal that he had connections to the armed forces.

He didn't even want to be here, but as he intended to permanently move to Denver, and under shifter law he was technically alpha of a pack of three, he was required to make his presence known to any powers in play, including the underworld.

The last thing he'd expected walking into this meeting was to see Savino order his own son beaten and then murder someone.

He could smell Quinn's anxiety and rage behind him, but he trusted Quinn not to interfere. As much as they both might loathe the situation, they didn't have any power here, much less authority.

Still, when Savino motioned for one of his men, who pulled out a gun and aimed it at the unconscious man, Caius couldn't stop himself from clearing his throat.

"If I may," he drawled, sipping the tea he'd been given as Savino eyed him. "If you intend to kill him, perhaps you'll let me take him off your hands instead." He felt Quinn's eyes boring into the back of his head, but he knew he didn't need to explain. They'd both seen far too many innocents die at the hands of those in power, and if he could finally save one, he'd do it. Not that he could prove the young man was innocent, but he'd put money on him being more upstanding than his father.

Savino made no effort to hide his distaste when he eyed Caius. "You ask me for my own son?"

Caius smiled faintly and set his tea down. "As you've just disowned him, I believe he belongs to no one, yes?"

He considered pressing further, but the sudden Spark of magic in the room made his breath catch. There was a mage here? Not just any mage, one who'd just come into their power, but he hadn't caught sight or scent of any children on the premises. No, when he followed the faint pull of magic, his gaze was drawn to the unconscious man on the floor.

Fuck. Savino's own son was a mage, and by the looks of it, not a single other person in this room besides him and Quinn realized it. As they were all human, that wasn't surprising. Shifters were far more sensitive to magic.

All the more reason to get his hands on Max. He may not have any sway in this city, but binding a mage to his pack before the Order found him would certainly change that.

He forced his heartbeat to calm and his face to show only mild interest. He couldn't risk revealing how much he wanted Max. If Caius couldn't get the mage out of here, Max would be better off dead than with the Order.

Savino grunted softly. "A trade then. You are looking to start a business in my city, yes? You take Max. You give me fifty percent of your earnings for five years."

Caius bristled. No way in the seven hells would he let the mob have a finger in his businesses. He pulled out his wallet with a hum and tossed a few grand on the table beside his cup. "I'm willing to buy him outright, but a half-dead man who's obviously suicidal isn't worth more than this."

Max was worth everything Caius had in the bank and then some, but only if he got hold of the mage first. Once everyone else realized what Max was, Caius wasn't sticking around for the war unless he had a binding in place.

He pushed his chair back and stood, buttoning his suit jacket. "I've made you aware of my pack's presence here. That's all I came to do." He tapped his fingers lightly against the cash. "Shall I leave this?"

Savino stared at him through narrowed eyes, too old and shrewd not to know there was a reason Caius wanted his son, but Caius hoped the old bastard assumed he was nothing more than a perverted shifter. Finally, Savino waved his hand with a scoff. "Take him. He is not worth the trouble anymore."

Caius nodded, restraining his fierce smirk of relief, and motioned for Quinn to retrieve Max.

As soon as they were out the door, he pulled his phone out, searching for the nearest independent mage healer. Thankfully, there was one in the city, though over half an hour away from them.

While Quinn got Max settled in the back seat, Caius slid into the passenger seat and put the address into the GPS. Once Quinn was behind the wheel, they were off.

"I can't believe you managed that," Quinn hissed as they sped out of the neighborhood and onto the main streets.

"Neither can I," he admitted, glancing back at Max, who was still unconscious. Not a good sign, but at least he wasn't leaking too much blood. "He's a bit old for his magic to Spark for the first time," he added quietly, turning back to watch the road.

"Maybe it was waiting for someone who could keep him safe to show up," Quinn said with a cheeky grin that Caius ignored. Quinn had made it clear he was a romantic from the first day they'd met, but Caius put no faith in higher powers.

He'd seen enough depravity to know that if gods did exist, they didn't give a fuck about the people they toyed with. Which was why he had to do everything in his power to ensure the safety of his pack. If that meant binding a new, untrained mage to them, he would.

By the time they reached the clinic, Max was starting to come around, but at Caius' request, the healer was kind enough to give him a potion that knocked him out again.

Caius stood at the end of the bed with his hands clasped behind his back, watching the healer work. At any moment, he expected the Order to show up, but even he knew they couldn't show up that quickly. And any independent mage would have ample shielding and protections in place. At least he hoped.

His eyes tracked the healer's familiar, a small white snake, as it slowly coiled around Max's body, guiding the healer to the most severe injuries. He held his tongue until she finally sat back with a soft sigh and turned her attention to Max's fingers.

"Can you put a block on him?" he asked, meeting the healer's suspicious look with a calm gaze.

"Why? If he's on the run—"

"His magic Sparked today."

Her eyes widened, and she turned back to Max.

"I'd like to ensure the Order doesn't force his hand."

With a soft swear and a wince, the healer shook her head. "He wouldn't survive them," she murmured. "But it'll cost extra."

"That's fine. Just get him back on his feet."

Convinced Max would make a full recovery, he left her to it and stepped out of the room, finding Quinn slouched in a chair with his phone. Caius stretched his senses past the doors, confirming no other mages were in the vicinity, before sinking into a chair next to Quinn. Since they'd rushed from Savino's place, he hadn't had the chance to confirm if Quinn had managed his part of the job.

He might have been required to make his pack's presence known, but he wouldn't pass up an opportunity to keep an eye on a criminal. "Did you get in?"

Quinn tipped his head back with a grin. "Of course," he said. "Their security was a joke. Whatever plans they make, we'll be able to see."

Caius nodded, some of his tension easing. He may have gone in with the vague intention of keeping an eye on Savino's operation for when and if Caius built a pack strong enough to challenge him, but for now, he was only interested in making sure Savino didn't have regrets about selling his son. Or at least not acting on them if he did.

"What are you going to tell Lukas?"

Caius let his head fall back with a groan, tempted to bash it into the wall. Lukas had served with him almost as long as Quinn, but he doubted the sniper would be happy to hear he'd swindled a mafia boss' son from him. Though he hoped the fact that the son was also a mage would be enough to appease him. He doubted it, but he could hope. "The truth, obviously," he said on a sigh.

Quinn laughed. "Good luck. Put him on speaker when you do. I wanna hear."

That wasn't going to happen. Considering Lukas was still dark from whatever mission he'd been sent on, Caius likely wouldn't get a chance to speak with him until he returned home. For now, he was more concerned with getting Max healed and settled so they could bind him before anyone else realized what he was.

Scan the QR Code
Below to Order!

SARIA BRYANT has been an avid reader since childhood and a fan fiction writer since middle school. They enjoy traveling and exploring and learning about other cultures and languages.

They are constantly dreaming up new ways to torment their characters and feeding a caffeine addiction.

Their favorite stories are M/M/+ relationships with a healthy dose of angst and drama with an HEA. When not reading or writing, they can usually be found watching anime or playing video games.

Saria can be found on Twitter/ Instagram / Tumblr / Bluesky @sariabryant.

Follow me on BookBub

SHADOW'S WOUND

ELEMENTAL THRONES
BOOK 1

❖ SARIA BRYANT ❖

With the realm teetering on the brink of magical annihilation, Callith Ratearynn, the reluctant heir to the Sun Throne, is thrust into power centuries too soon. With his father dead and corruption tearing the kingdom apart at the seams, Cal must battle rising racial tensions and unravel a dark conspiracy. Justice, a manipulative human official, has stirred hatred between humans and the magical community, using enslavement collars and control over the Black Sun—an elite group of soldiers loyal to the Shadow Throne.

Just as civil war seems inevitable, Cal's Fate string—a magical bond tying him to his soulmate—leads him to a grim prison where he finds Haru, his bonded, broken and tortured. But Fate has more in store. Cal discovers he is bound not to one, but two: Rashi, a fox shifter, and Haru, a fierce dragon warrior. Together, this reluctant triad must face cult attacks, dark rituals, and the creeping Wound, a void threatening to consume their realm.

Cal's new reality is one of impossible choices—between duty and heart, loyalty and passion. As war looms, the only hope lies in Cal's ability to trust in his newfound soulmates and uncover the depths of the corruption before it's too late.

SCAN THE QR CODE
BELOW TO ORDER!

WILD'S SCAR

ELEMENTAL THRONES
BOOK II

SARIA BRYANT

Vesryn Rydel has a new Fate string—a magical bond tying him to his soulmate. Unfortunately it's to a fae who lost all memory of his name to the human who enslaved him. He gives himself the name Fey: Fated to die.

Neither want a Fate bond—Vesryn because he is a guard to the heir of the Sun Throne, and Fey because he must venture north to seal the veil between realms that ripped open with his return.

On their journey through the Wound—the barren, magic-void, lifeless wasteland that tore across the center of their continent—they must learn to trust each other and accept the memories of their past selves in order to restore both the Wild Throne and balance to their world.

Packed full of magic and mystery, *Wild's Scar* is the stunning sequel to *Shadow's Wound*.

SCAN THE QR CODE
BELOW TO ORDER!

If You

LET ME

TOUCH OF LEATHER ·BOOK 1·

SARIA BRYANT

When Jasper is invited by his cousin to a kink club, he's all too eager for a chance to try something new, especially when Vincent, a gorgeous man in a suit, offers to bring his fantasy to life. After an amazing scene together and his first true taste of kink, Jasper is hooked. What starts as a one-night-a-week exploration quickly turns into a request for more and a contract between them.

Having given up on finding a sub for himself after his last disaster of a relationship, Vincent is surprised to find himself drawn to Jasper. More than the contradiction of shy young man and bratty personality, Jasper seems made specifically to submit to Vincent. Their chemistry is amazing, and Vincent is willing to try again. The only problem is Jasper's self-doubt and near-desperate need to please.

SCAN THE QR CODE
BELOW TO ORDER!

Oathsworn

Can love set a
mage free?

Sebastian Black

CharmD
Saga

Can love set a mage free?

Former chef Jasper Wight has been magically ensnared in his apartment for over three months. *Cabin fever* doesn't begin to cover it. All he can do to pass the time is indulge in his hobby—painting portraits of his neighbors. But once a handsome new man moves into a swanky nearby penthouse, Jasper is no longer content merely to watch. Following his gut, he reaches out through astral projection….

Finn Anderson is the CEO of a food app funded by his parents, but he struggles to believe in the dream. When a mysterious someone starts leaving messages on his mirror, he learns the world holds more possibilities than he ever imagined.

When a chance encounter brings Finn to Jasper's door, the pair are soon as enamored with each other as Finn is of the magic he's just discovering. But navigating a relationship that spans two worlds is only the tip of the iceberg. They still have to figure out how to free Jasper from his apartment, how to make Finn's business into a success, and whether an outsider can be trusted with the secrets of the magical world.

SCAN THE QR CODE
BELOW TO ORDER!

AMY LANE

Sometimes the
best magic is just
a little luck…

THE
RISING TIDE

THE LUCK MECHANICS BOOK ONE

The tidal archipelago of Spinner's Drift is a refuge for misfits. Can the island's magic help a pie-in-the-sky dreamer and a wounded soul find a home in each other?

In a flash of light and a clap of thunder, Scout Quintero is banished from his home. Once he's sneaked his sister out too, he's happy, but their power-hungry father is after them, and they need a place to lie low. The thriving resort business on Spinner's Drift provides the perfect way to blend in.

They aren't the only ones who think so.

Six months ago Lucky left his life behind and went on the run from mobsters. Spinner's Drift brings solace to his battered soul, but one look at Scout and he's suddenly terrified of having one more thing to lose.

Lucky tries to keep his distance, but Scout is charming, and the island isn't that big. When they finally connect, all kinds of things come to light, including supernatural mysteries that have been buried for years. But while working on the secret brings Scout and Lucky closer, pissed-off mobsters, supernatural entities, and Scout's father are getting closer to *them*. Can they hold tight to each other and weather the rising tide together?

SCAN THE QR CODE
BELOW TO ORDER!